'He's the Giant Irish Wolf, boss,' said Sam. 'The only one left in the world, I'm told.'

The great John L. Rutherford got quite a thrill as he looked at Finn. He'd lost one of his lions recently and felt the menagerie lacked something really fierce. Like Sam, he'd never heard of a Wolfhound or seen a dog of this size and strength. To anyone who didn't know him or realise the circumstances that had brought on this fierceness, there's no doubt that Finn was an awe-inspiring and magnificent sight. His cage was two metres high, yet Finn's feet came within centimetres of the roof as he plunged at the partition between him and the tiger. Crouching in the corner, as though about to spring, his black eyes blazed fire and fury.

Finn the Wolfhound

A. J. Dawson

Abridged by Alexander Swaby

Hodder
Children's
Books

a division of Hodder Headline plc

A catalogue record for this title is available from the British Library.

Typesetting by Phoenix Typesetting, Ilkley, West Yorkshire.

Printed and bound in Great Britain by
Cox & Wyman Ltd, Reading, Berkshire.

Hodder Children's Books
a division of Hodder Headline plc
338 Euston Road
London NW1 3BH

Contents

1

The Mother of Heroes

For a man not much older than thirty, his face was worn, suggesting he felt life's difficulties more than he should.

He rose from his desk, straightening his back with a long sigh. Stretching both arms over his shoulders, he crossed the little room to the window. Through the driving sleet he had an extensive view of dully gleaming roofs and chimneypots.

The man turned from the bleak February day and looked round his den. The walls that weren't covered by bookshelves had an odd mixture of pictures of men, women and dogs. While the people were mostly authors, the dogs were, without exception, Irish Wolfhounds – fine animals combining the speed of the greyhound, the strength of the boarhound and the picturesque shagginess of the deerhound. From Christian times, these animals had been friends and companions to kings, chieftains and mighty hunters.

For several minutes he gazed at a girl with wind-blown hair, a happy face and laughing eyes. The 'Mistress of the Kennels' as the picture was named, was standing in a wide kennel enclosure with a small puppy in her arms. Behind, the land sloped away to meadows. The man then looked at pictures of various Irish Wolfhounds, each inscribed with the name and age of the dog.

Sighing once more, he returned to the window. As he stared out, the door opened and the girl in the photo entered. Her face was not quite the same as it had been but her eyes still laughed. Seeing his expression she said, 'Yes, it is rather, isn't it? After Croft.'

'Don't talk to me of Croft,' the man replied, 'or you'll bring on my spring madness before its time. It's two years and four months since we left Croft and that open life we had. I was looking at the "Mistress of the Kennels". Do you remember?'

'Oh, yes. It was just after Tara's illness. It's a blessing the old dear has such a lovely home in Devon, isn't it?'

'It could have been much worse and I shouldn't be unhappy – but two and a half years! I wanted to be sure we'd really be able to stay without running back to town with our tails between our legs. All the same, when I look out of that window – what I'd give for a cottage.'

'But cottages don't have kennels. At least not Wolf-hound kennels.'

'I know. It would be quite mad. But I thought I felt the spring madness this morning as I looked through the window.'

'Oh, well. Do you know why I came in? It's the last day of the Dog Show. I thought it might be a good idea for you to take time off and go there while I'm out this afternoon. If you don't it'll be the third year you've missed.'

'I would have thought a dog show was a dangerous thing for spring madness,' the man replied with a strange little smile.

'Quite right. A trial of strength. Besides, it would do you good to meet the people. Do go.'

An hour later he was on his way to the Dog Show where, in earlier years, he had been one of the principal exhibitors. A bout of ill-health had cut his earnings but not his over-generous nature. Eventually he'd been forced to sell his country home with the kennels and stables and move to London where he could live more economically while increasing his earnings.

Parting with his dogs had been heartbreaking. Had it not been for the excellent home offered in Devon, he might have been tempted to take Tara, the mother of heroes, with him, despite the lack of space. The lady who bought Tara from her Master had been very keen to have her. So much so that as well as a lovely home she promised faithfully never to part with Tara except back to her Master.

On the day Tara left for her new home, her Master was feeling very bad about the whole thing. The household gathered to say goodbye to the beautiful hound and then the Master himself took her to the station. From the guard's van she looked through the barred window at her friend. Afterwards, he said it had taken every ounce of self control not to jump on board and release her.

But glowing reports were received of Tara in her new home with its extensive gardens. So, while Tara was never forgotten, her Master no longer grieved over her.

Arriving at the Dog Show he wandered between the benches, stopping now and then to speak to old friends – human and canine. Being the last day, most exhibitors had left, giving the place a dismal air.

Presently he found himself in an outbuilding where an auction was being held. Sitting by the side of the ring he watched the dogs parade. After a while a young Irish Wolfhound entered, immediately catching the Master's eye. It was one he had bred at Croft. He inspected the dog with great interest and was describing its merits to a group of buyers when he felt another dog nuzzle his arm and wrist. But the Master was too engrossed in the young dog to notice.

At last the youngster was led away and the auctioneer announced:

'Now ladies and gentlemen it's the turn of lot 127. A magnificent bitch by the famous Champion O'Leary. Come on man, let's have the dog in the ring.'

An attendant close by the Master tugged at a chain. The Master had been deep in conversation but turned in response to the persistent nuzzling of the unseen animal.

'Just push her out, sir, will you?' asked the harassed attendant. 'I can't get her to budge. She's as strong as a mule.'

'Let me have the chain,' said the Master, 'I expect you're frightened . . . Why! Tara! Tara, dear old lady. Who the devil put this hound in here?'

'Mrs Forsyth, the owner,' said the groom, forcing his way through the crowd.

The Master wasted a few minutes, but not many, mentally protesting Mrs Forsyth's underhanded actions. The Master fondled Tara's head as she stood erect with her front paws on his shoulders. For ten acutely unhappy minutes she had nuzzled her friend's hand without a hint of recognition or response. But now her noble face was alight with gladness and love.

The Master walked to the auctioneer, followed by Tara who effortlessly dragged her attendant behind without the slightest heed to his angry jerks on her collar.

'I'm sorry sir,' said the auctioneer after a moment's conversation. 'I can't possibly postpone the sale. The owner's instructions are that the dog must definitely be sold. No, there's no reserve. Yes, I can take your cheque as deposit, providing you get it endorsed by the Show Secretary. Very well, sir, five minutes.'

Five minutes was not much time, but he couldn't see Tara sold in the ring to a dealer. The groom had said Mrs Forsyth was in the tea-room and, angrily, he went to look for her. Back and forth he hurried through the noisy building, with no success. At the Secretary's office he obtained clearance for his cheque, while at the same time bitterly realising that he would never be able to afford the price Tara would bring. Finally, on being told that Mrs Forsyth had left the building, he hurried back to the ring, catching a glimpse of the lovely Tara, standing sorrowfully and stately as a man in a kennel-coat bid forty-eight guineas.

'Forty-nine!' cried the Master through tight lips.

Just then the ferrety face of a well-known, low grade dealer thrust from the crowd. He had a bad reputation for overcrowding Danes and Newfoundlands in a miserable East London backyard. Several times he'd been ordered out of show rings for malpractice. Although he'd never owned Wolfhounds, he was smart enough to spot profit when he saw it and nodded to the auctioneer.

'Fifty guineas I'm bid for this celebrated Wolfhound bitch, dam of many champions. Fifty-one guineas. Is this my last . . .'

The auctioneer babbled on. The price was already way beyond what the Master could afford.

The ferrety dealer raised the bid to fifty-three and the Master bit his lip as he made it fifty-four.

'May I say fifty-five?' the auctioneer asked the man in the kennel-coat. 'Come on ladies and gentlemen. Time and tide and auctioneers wait for no man. The hammer is about to fall at fifty-four guineas. Going once. Thank you sir!' – to the dealer – 'I'm bid fifty-five guineas only for this noble animal. What about you sir, who the dog seems to recognise? Surely such devotion deserves a little recognition?'

'We're not dealing in personalities,' snapped the Master, turning on his heel. 'Sixty guineas!'

The auctioneer smiled. 'As you say, sir. This is business. Sixty guineas – and one. Seventy guineas to the man in the kennel-coat.'

The Master turned slowly and left the ring, following the ferret-faced dealer, who'd dropped out at sixty-one. He daren't offer more but couldn't bear to see Tara led away by a stranger.

'Going, going, gone!'

Once more in the main building he moodily lit a pipe and wondered what to do. He had to find the buyer so he could pass on one or two of Tara's whims and peculiarities in the hope that she might get more consideration in her new home. Across the dusty, littered hall, he could see an elderly lady leading Tara. In a moment he recognised the lady as an old friend from Yorkshire who had bought two of his whelps. And here she was, walking straight towards him. Bending down, she unhooked Tara's chain. In an instant the great hound bounded forward to her beloved friend, nuzzling him furiously and then standing against his shoulders. Her soft eyes glistened, brimming with love and delight. The man's eyes weren't altogether dry either as he growled affectionate nonsense into her silky ears.

'Tara knows her real friends,' said the Yorkshire lady, shaking hands with the Master. 'Please take her chain and never give anyone the right to handle it. You'll allow me this pleasure I'm sure, if only for the love I have for Tara's son. I know Mrs Forsyth well. She has fads and changes her pets as often as her gloves. I couldn't possibly let a stranger buy the mother of my Dhulert. So, it gives me real pleasure to be the means of bringing her to you once more.'

Catching a glimpse of his expression, the silver-haired woman lowered her eyes as the Master grasped her hands. He tried but no words could express his gratitude.

Tara and he walked all the way home, twice making long detours for the sake of solitude and the feel of open grass, despite it being sooty and soaked. They swapped remarks and Tara kept putting dollops of London mud on his shoulders. At last they came to the mansions. They crept close to the railings, dodging quickly through the entrance to avoid being seen from above. Dogs were not supposed to be kept at all, so the idea of a Wolfhound eighty centimetres high would have been preposterous. But at that moment, the Master cared nothing for the rules.

The meeting between Tara and the Mistress of the Kennels was a joy to see. The flat seemed ridiculously tiny with Tara inside. But, although large, she was also extremely graceful and managed to move around without so much as brushing a chair leg. There was great rejoicing and much planning the night the mother of heroes returned to the friends who had watched over her since birth.

2

In the beginning

Tara cared little about the lack of space. All she wanted was to stretch out her long body on the hearth-rug, and gaze at her friend through the forest of overgrown eyebrows which screened her soft, brown eyes. In any event, too many changes occurred during the next four months to leave much time for considering the size of her quarters.

Within a few days of the Dog Show, Tara was taken on a two day visit to a farm in Oxfordshire. Here, she renewed her acquaintance with Champion Dermot Asthore. He was one of the aristocrats of her race and father of the fine young hounds she had given to the world.

After that, something considerable seemed to happen every day. The Master spoke laughingly about the spring madness and of great profit to furniture removers. The Master laughed a good deal and took Tara and the Mistress with him on his many journeys from Victoria railway station.

Then came a day of extraordinary confusion; men in aprons marched through the flat, turning furniture upside down and made foolish remarks about Tara. That night, she slept in a loose box in a country inn, and in the morning went out for a glorious run on the Downs with the Master, who seemed to have grown younger since they left London.

Within a few days Tara and her friends had settled comfortably into their new home. It was an odd-shaped little house, full of unexpected angles and doors. A garden and orchard staggered up the lower slope of one of the

Downs. There was a rather poky stable but an excellent coach house; light and airy with a new concrete floor which the Master had helped to lay. The back half of the coach house had a raised platform – ideal for lying in the spring sunshine flooding the room.

Between the stable and the house was a big, wooden structure, as large as a barn but with an ordinary-sized door. The inside was comfortably panelled in wood and it soon became the Master's den. The bookshelves were mounted along one wall with the Master's collection of photographs. A big stove was added to warm the place, and just beyond the desk a two metre square platform was built, with sides about fifteen centimetres high. Tara watched the Master first cover this platform with pleasant smelling sawdust, and over that, nailing down a tightly stretched piece of carpet, making an altogether excellent bed. During the day, Tara preferred to lie by the Master's desk or on a rug by the door where the sunshine formed a pool of warmth and light. Here it was that Tara took her meals; a dish of milk in the morning, with a little bread or biscuit, and her main meal of the day, always prepared by the Mistress of the Kennels.

As time went by, Tara became less active. Beyond the orchard there were plenty of rabbits to chase, but lately the Master was discouraging her. Gradually she lost interest in the sport, except when greatly tempted by a rabbit springing out from under her nose.

In the afternoons, when she went out with the Mistress, Tara generally wore a lead on her collar, to ensure a steady pace at all times. Without knowing why, Tara had the contented feeling that these precautions were wise. She felt the same about her meals, always drinking her morning milk, even when she didn't feel like it, licking the dish dry with her great, red tongue. She could not have explained any of this, but subconscious knowledge and instinct play a large part in a Wolfhound's life.

But it wasn't just in the avoidance of violent exercise that Tara's instinct guided her. One morning, as she strolled along the shrubbery, it occurred to Tara that it might be a good thing to dig a hole somewhere – a sort of cave where she could find shelter if need be. As Tara forced herself between two shrubs and began excavating, the Master watched with a sympathetic smile of understanding. The earth was soft and moist, and Tara's powerful front paws scooped out shovelfuls for her hind paws to scatter in an earthy rain.

Once she'd finished her cavern, Tara divided the rest of the day between the den and the coach house. Lying at ease, with one eye on the Master, she wondered vaguely why she'd bothered to dig the hole. But the Master knew and seemed quite satisfied.

The next day Tara inspected the hole and decided it wasn't good enough. She found a more secluded spot and dug a second cave. Then, Tara toured the entire premises, visiting various places where she'd hidden bones over the past two weeks.

The following day Tara was restless and unhappy. She had a nagging feeling she'd forgotten something important that required her attention. In an effort to remember, she dug two or three more holes, and then buried one of the Master's slippers in a ditch; something she'd never done before. The thought of burying such a precious piece of property troubled Tara but she couldn't bring herself to return it, so great was the drive to hoard treasure.

During the afternoon her uneasiness increased. Fifty times, the Master opened and shut the door to suit her whim. Tara felt ashamed but simply couldn't settle. After dinner she was given some warm olive oil; an odd but generally pleasing thing to take, she thought. Waking from a short doze, Tara had the sudden urge to tear a hole in the carpet on her bed. She felt pleased with herself, having remembered this job in good time, and was disappointed when the Master prevented her. He held her paws and gently lowered Tara on to her side.

A cart stopped outside the house. A hint of an odour drifted into the room, causing the hound's nose to wrinkle ominously. With a savage bark, Tara sprang to her feet. She was unsure what ailed her, but was conscious of a great anger and passionate hostility. The Master calmed her and carefully locked her in the den, before making his way round the house to take delivery of a large hamper. The Mistress of the Kennels sat with Tara, while the Master busied himself in the coach house with the hamper, a lantern and a milky, sloppy sort of dog's dinner.

It was a strange and eventful night in the den. All around was as silent as the grave, and the soft June air was as sweet as rose petals. The Mistress was persuaded to go to bed early, but the Master sat writing at his desk. He got up now and then to peep into the raised bed in the shadow. Just after the village clock struck one, the Master was thrilled to hear a cry from Tara; the fifth he'd heard in three and a half hours.

He leaned forward on his elbows to watch. Tara knew nothing of self-control, but that cry of hers was the only self-indulgence she showed before busying herself with utmost delicacy over the care of her latest offspring; the last in a family of five. At the same moment, a weak bleating cry could be heard, not at all like Tara's voice, but pleasing to the Master all the same.

With infinite care, Tara lowered her great bulk in a coil on the bed, around four glossy Wolfhound puppies, now perfectly sheltered against their mother's flank. Blindly grovelling over the carpet bed in different directions, they had been nudged and nuzzled into place so Tara could lower her pain-racked body to rest. One inch of miscalculation and the life would have been crushed from those tiny bodies.

A quick look satisfied the mother that the four were safe. Then, without a thought of rest, she manoeuvred the newcomer between her front paws and gave it the life-giving and stimulating tongue wash. Over and over the little grey bundle was turned, cheeping and bleating in protest, until every nook and cranny of its soft body had been swept by Tara's tenderly rough, long tongue. The mother's sensitive nose coaxed the little creature towards his sisters and brothers already nestling against her flank. They continued to feed busily from her swollen teats and were completely indifferent to an addition to their number.

Only then did the mother drop her head on her paws, drawing a long breath of relief. A moment later, overcoming her tiredness, Tara glanced at the Master who was aware of her every move. He brought over a dish of cool water which Tara lapped weakly but gratefully. The man bent over slowly and carefully examined the litter.

'There, there Tara my girl,' he crooned, fetching a dish of warm milk and water. Tara drank eagerly, though she was constrained in her movements for fear of disturbing the little ones.

After just ten minutes, the mother's rest was over. First she licked her teats and then the featureless faces of the pups. Within minutes they were once more driven by hunger; with wriggling tails, impatient feet thrust out and wet gaping jaws, they were nursing in a row like clockwork.

With pride in her eyes, Tara turned towards her friend before sinking into a few more minutes of well-earned rest.

'Good girl,' whispered the Master, 'five is a very good number. You don't want a big litter, do you, girl? Besides, that last one is equal to any two I ever saw.'

The Master lay down and slept too. In the June daylight he verified his opinion of the last born as a grey-brindle, the biggest whelp of his age he'd ever seen. For purposes of the Kennel Club registration, the Mistress named him Finn, in honour of the fourth century warrior Irish Wolfhound considered by King Cormac to be the chief of the household and his most honoured counsellor.

On that first morning, Finn was no bigger than a kitten and could rest easily on the Master's palm. But he was a direct descendant of King Cormac's battle hounds of 1,500 years ago, and had the makings of being the biggest Wolfhound ever bred.

3

The foster-mother

Finn's first adventure occurred when he was no more than thirty-seven hours old and still as blind as a bat. It was to affect the rest of his life.

Finn was asleep, snug between his mother's hind legs, on the great bed in the den. When pups are lying with their mother, there's always one spot that's cosier than the rest. You might think that these shapeless little bundles would have no more intelligence than a potato, but from the very beginning, the best place was exclusively occupied by Finn. Even if one of the others crawled over Finn in his sleep, the moment he awoke the interloper would be rolled backwards, protesting futilely, only for Finn to regain his chosen spot. Whatever was best, in food, warmth or comfort, Finn would claim, even at this absurdly young age, by virtue of his greater strength and vitality.

As Finn and the rest slept and Tara dozed, the Master came in and spoke invitingly. The great bitch rose carefully, causing the pups to roll helplessly on their backs, cheeping for something, even if they didn't realise just what. In his masterful way, Finn burrowed under his brothers and sisters to benefit from their warmth. A quick maternal glance saw that all was well and Tara followed the Master out into the sunlight.

'Come and see the Mistress, old lady, and stretch yourself.'

Tara strolled round the yard. Then, without much appetite, she lapped conscientiously at a dish of warm milk and bread which the Mistress had provided in her kitchen.

When the dish was almost finished, Tara suddenly realised the Master was missing. Searching quickly left and right, Tara bounded for the door.

'Look out for Tara,' cried the Mistress, through an open window.

'All right, I'm clear now,' replied the Master, from beyond the gate leading to the coach house. 'Let her in now, will you.'

The Mistress opened the house door and in three cat-like strides, Tara reached the den, and stood on her hind legs with her forepaws against the door – about two metres above the ground.

'There, there pet, your children are all right, you'll see,' said the Mistress, letting her into the den.

In an instant, Tara was in the midst of her pups, still bunched and snugly asleep. Tara looked gratefully at the Mistress as the pups mewed around her feet. Tara coiled into position for them to nurse, apparently totally unaware that now there were only four mouths feeding instead of five. Whether or not Tara realised that Finn was missing is impossible to say. In any event, four gaping mouths and wriggling bodies was plenty to look after. And if she did notice that the big grey whelp was missing, she was too devoted a mother to risk injuring the remaining four by fretting over matters outside her immediate control.

Once Tara was settled comfortably, the Mistress hurried back to the house in time to see the Master unwrapping little Finn from a soft blanket. He placed him among three puppies perhaps half his size, in a hamper by the stove. Finn bleated half-heartedly for a minute or two and then, full of milk and very warm, forgot what the trouble was and drifted off to sleep.

Closing the hamper lid the Master said: 'I'll let him have two good hours there. Finn ought to take on the smell of the others pretty well by then. What do you think of the foster?'

'Oh, I like her,' said the Mistress of the Kennels. 'She seems nice and affectionate and seems to have recovered from her awful journey. I think she'll make a good mother. She seems to have plenty of milk – more than is comfortable for her, poor little thing.'

'Yes. Exactly what I want. If she's uncomfortable, she's less likely to resent Finn's intrusion.'

'You've decided then to put Finn to a foster-mother?'

'Yes. Poor old Tara – well, she . . .'

'I know. She's poor old spoiled Tara.'

The Master chuckled. 'Well perhaps that's partly it. But she deserves it. The old girl has done her share of prize-winning and nursing. Think of her as a lady that's earned a rest, particularly . . .'

'Particularly after her illness. Yes, I know.'

'Four pups are plenty. I still think that the mammitis permanently affected her heart – and other things. I'm not sure we shouldn't have taken them all from her.'

'But why choose Finn to be fostered?' asked the Mistress, thoughtfully balancing on her finger the wooden spoon used to mix Tara's meals.

'Well, that's rather an interesting point. I know you think that Tara is everything a Wolfhound should be. But a mongrel's milk is stronger. It's heartier food than Tara's aristocrat blood can produce. Also, by giving the foster just one pup, when she's probably capable of rearing two or three, that one should do exceedingly well. Finn is an exception and I want to give him every chance of growing into the largest Wolfhound living. Unless I'm mistaken, in a week he'll be the fattest tub of a pup in all England.'

After an hour Finn woke and set off in the vain search for his mother's milk, trampling over his bedfellows, bleating all the while. But soon the warmth of the kitchen sent him off to sleep once more.

An hour later, Finn's furious lungs made it clear he would let nothing stand between him and a good square meal. Several times Finn thought he'd found a teat, and the blind fury he displayed on realising he was chewing on a comrade's muzzle was quite terrifying. Spluttering,

Finn would lose his balance and roll on to his back, four pink feet wriggling in a passion of protest.

It was in this undignified position that the Master found him. Chuckling, he picked Finn up and wrapped him in a warm blanket with two of the other pups. The third pup was handed over to the gardener.

The next thing Finn knew was his gaping mouth being held against something soft and exuding warm milk. Immediately, his little hind legs began to work like pistons while his front paws kneaded and pounded the soft udder. Finn and his foster-brothers were feeding from the soft-eyed sheepdog, comfortably occupying a corner of the large bed in the coach house. She was very glad to lose some of her excess milk and curved her body to make it easier for the pups to feed.

The Master leaned forward to watch the foster-mother lick the back of the nearest dog – one of her own. As her sensitive nose passed over the first pup to Finn's wriggling tail, her eyes hardened. Looking straight down her muzzle, she saw the stranger's fat, grey back, twice the size of her own. No warm tongue caressed this one; instead, an unsympathetic nose pushed him spluttering away, right off the bed.

Almost before Finn's wet mouth began to protest, the Master put him back to the warm teats. Again the suspicious nose checked Finn's tail; this time a low resentful growl followed. Finn instinctively wriggled from under the cold nose while his mouth and forepaws searched for food. Before the threatened bite came, the Master gently pressed the sheepdog's head down on the straw.

His hand remained there until the three pups were comfortably full and the foster was eased of her bountiful milk supply. Then he gently removed his hand and allowed the foster to lick her puppies, although she politely refused to clean the stranger. In due course, when Finn plodded around her neck with the arrogance of a well-fed youngster, she turned her head in the opposite direction and gave him the cold shoulder. The Master petted her and gave her a little warm milk and bread before taking the pups away in a warm blanket. One of them was handed to someone in the kitchen. Finn, with one sleepy foster-brother, was placed in the hamper near the stove.

A couple of hours later, the foster-mother began to worry and hope her family would come again to feed. At the same time, Finn and his friend wished they could have another meal. Ten minutes later, the Master put them to nurse once more. Once or twice, by accident, the foster-mother brushed Finn with her tongue, but she didn't growl.

'Good,' observed the Master, filling his pipe as he sat on a nearby barrel.

The natural order of things for puppies is to feed, grovel and wriggle to sleep, then to begin the cycle all over again. During this period the mother cleans her offspring. For several minutes the true son was given a good licking, but Finn was once again ignored.

The bitch closed her eyes. Finn, ready for some fun, straddled the dog's nose and pressed his round tummy against her nostrils, wriggling helplessly. The Master leaned forward, ready to snatch Finn from danger but a curious thing happened. The sheepdog growled and Finn toppled over in alarm. Even as she growled though, her maternal instincts came to his rescue. She rolled Finn back on to his feet and then gave him the comforting licking and tongue wash his body needed. Feeling much more content, when the wash was over, Finn sidled up to his companion and in a minute the pair of them were asleep.

The Master laid down his pipe and for a few minutes stroked and fondled the bitch, chatting all the while, establishing a bond between them.

The next morning, while being petted and fed in the garden, someone removed the foster-mother's own puppy. When she returned to the coach house, full of contentment after a good meal, some exercise and plenty of petting, she found the bed was occupied only by the big, grey whelp. But her surprise was short-lived and within minutes she was happily giving him his morning wash and polish.

Afterwards, she lay down in such a fashion that Finn could feed easily while she was able to watch the rise and fall of his chubby body from the corner of her eye.

The sturdy sheepdog proved to be a kind and diligent foster-mother to Finn. Just as well, for the Master and Mistress were preoccupied with Tara's health. Her puppies were thin and delicate while she herself was only just saved by constant care and attention and the latest medicines. The Master decided to arrange for another foster-mother, but less than an hour after she had arrived, one of Tara's pups died. Concern for Tara deepened. The Master felt that if the illness re-occurred it would be fatal, and he spent hours staving it off. A local carpenter quickly made a bed for the foster-mother in a shed in the orchard. The crossbred spaniel soon regained lost ground for the remaining pups.

Finn, in the coach house, knew nothing of all this. He was still totally blind and pampered beyond his wildest dreams, with all the food and care he could ever hope for. With only one whelp to look after, the foster-mother never lost sight of her charge. If he did happen to stray away from the warmth of her body at night, the sheepdog's instinct soon woke her to nose her erring infant back to sleep and warmth and safety.

When the Master looked in on the night of the tenth day, he was surprised to find that Finn's eyes were still showing no signs of opening. By now, he was feeling easy about Tara who appeared almost recovered. She spent her days lying in the den having apparently forgotten her illness and her puppies.

'Perhaps it's as well he's still blind, for your sake,' the Master chatted to the foster-mother. 'He'll lead you a merry dance before long, I should imagine. Never mind, old girl, you must do the best that you can for Finn; he's a great pup.'

Great he certainly was, sprawling across the little sheepdog's sandy flank. Finn took up pretty well as much space as the whole of her litter would have done. His pink pads looked monstrous. His legs were twice the thickness you'd have expected. And his fat shapeless body was very nearly as wide as it was long. Finn's flat black nose at the end of an unusually long, black, marked muzzle, was remarkably broad, something which pleased the Master who had long studied Wolfhounds. Between the black 'corners' of Finn's body – the tip of his tail, feet and face – his colour was a steely grey.

On the twelfth morning, sunlight in the coach house stirred the sheepdog. She yawned and stretched, waking Finn in the process. Instantly he burrowed his head in search of food, emerging some minutes later with milk on his snout. Nosed into place, Finn was given his morning wash and brush. The licking ended, the mother stretched and decided on a stroll. Finn rolled rollickingly on his back, then staggered on to his absurdly large feet. He backed sideways like a crab and then tried to rub an eye with one of his massive paws, but fell plump on his nose. Staggering back up on to his feet he faced the broad sunbeam, dividing the coach house. Then, as though tried beyond endurance, he opened his jaws wide and bleated his fear and distress to the world. The patient foster-mother cut short her walk and hopped back to his aid, comforting him with her tongue and odd, throaty sounds.

For several minutes the pup refused to be comforted. An hour or so later, when the Master dropped in, he understood at a glance what the trouble was. Finn had been given a real shock, his distress lasting some thirty minutes. But soon afterwards, his youthful curiosity took over once more. He was suddenly aware of being blind no longer; he had stepped, at one stride, into a seeing life.

He spent practically all of the day testing this new sense. He found that if he crawled away from his foster-mother the air became whiter and whiter until, at last, he stubbed his nose. As well as walls, in the other direction he found a ledge a few centimetres high. With a huge effort, Finn hoisted himself up only to find the floor rush up and hit him hard, leaving him helpless on his back until his foster-mother patiently lifted him in her jaws back on to the bed.

From this point onwards, Finn progressed rapidly, quickly developing his own masterful personality. He was still only when he slept. He grovelled diligently all through his waking hours, until his podgy legs had hardened sufficiently to carry his bulk and, despite many falls, he began scurrying around on his feet. He'd take two to four jerky strides, like some fussy old gentleman trying to catch a train, before subsiding in a confused heap, on chest or nose, his tail wagging angrily in mid-air. This was not so annoying as you might think. For although he was stopped suddenly in mid-stream, it seemed reasonable enough as he'd already forgotten where he was heading.

During his third week the weather was particularly fine. Finn and the other pups spent long periods sunbathing in a small, fenced-off square of gravel, which was covered with deodorised sawdust. These periods were fun for the pups and relaxing for both foster-mothers. Although they were never allowed to see each other they were both within smelling distance of their pups.

On the twenty-first morning, Finn spent half an hour on the Mistress's lap, learning to lap warm milk and water. First he learned to suck the milky tip of her little finger. Then she gradually guided his nose along her finger into the milk. One way or another, he managed about a tablespoon of milk in that first lesson. The same afternoon, he was kept from the foster-mother for two and a half hours, during which time he and the other pups made great progress in the art of lapping; although they still approached their feeding seriously when returned to their mother. Still they were beginning to learn, and in succeeding days some became experts. Finn's trouble was over enthusiasm and he risked suicide by plunging his whole face in the milk.

In the fourth week the milk was fortified with cereals rich in nutrients and it became a real meal. At the end of the fifth week the pups were solemnly weighed on the kitchen scales. The record showed that his sisters and brothers weighed from four and a half kilograms to six kilograms, while Finn weighed over a kilogram more.

In other words, although still only five weeks old, Finn weighed as much as a full-grown fox terrier and was the same size. After corresponding with other breeders, the Master was more certain than ever that Finn was a maker and breaker of records.

For the next week Finn's meals included broth as well as milky foods. He visited his foster-mother only once during the day to feed, although he was still allowed to sleep with her at night. All four pups played together in the orchard from six in the morning till six at night, a twig or leaf becoming a fierce enemy to stalk or fight with noisy recklessness.

Life was sweet on the Sussex Downs. The sun shone warmly and life was very good – if only one didn't lose one's breath so quickly and find one's legs buckling annoyingly at the wrong moment. What was that rascally fawn pup rushing for? The Mistress with the four little dishes? Another meal? Bother, I should certainly have reached her first, if only I hadn't somersaulted over my brother.

That was how life seemed to Finn – one long playtime. And yet there were glimpses of a more serious side; that night he discovered he could bark, like grown up dogs. True, the force of barking upset his balance, causing him to land on his side. But he soon learned to prop himself against a table leg where he watched with amazement at the paralysing effect his voice had on the others who sat round respectfully watching him. They had all yapped before, but now one in three of Finn's barks had a deep powerful ring. After a while, his sister came and chewed Finn's back with some vague idea that the sound came from there.

When Finn was led to the coach house that night, he decided to show the little sheepdog what he'd learned. Swaggering unsteadily, he gave three loud barks of varying pitches. The sheepdog, less than twice Finn's size now, looked up from her food and barked back just as vigorously. Finn sniffed casually at her plate whereupon the bitch growled ferociously and shouldered him away. The Master nodded thoughtfully.

'Yes,' he said, as Finn sidled off to his bed, rather crestfallen, 'I think you should take that as your notice to quit, my son. That's weaning for you. I think this is your last night as a baby.'

And that was the last Finn saw of his foster-mother. That was the end of babyhood and the beginning of childhood for Finn.

4

Youth beside the Downs

Finn had only one night by himself on the great bed in the coach house. The next night the other three puppies joined him. They whimpered a little at the loss of their mother's comfort, giving Finn the opportunity to swagger around after the previous night's experience. He'd already adopted the air of someone accustomed to getting his own way. He let it be known that he was master and that no one should encroach on any space he claimed as his own. All day long, the four of them played in the orchard. If it rained, the Mistress bustled them into the shed, which was always open and where most of their meals were served.

Sixteen days after Finn had been first weighed he'd put on almost half as much again. Growth of around a quarter of a kilogram a day requires wise feeding and care. At twenty weeks Finn weighed forty-four kilograms. Puppies' legs are easily bowed and rarely straightened so Finn and his family were never allowed on damp ground and were seldom out of sight of the Master or Mistress of the Kennels for more than half an hour.

Life for the pups was a delightfully haphazard affair. A lot of play mixed with eating and sleeping and, for excitement, the odd mock-fight over the huge bones given to them as toothbrush and tooth sharpener. They loved to dig holes or hide behind trees before springing out with blood curdling cries. Finn like nothing better than galloping down the orchard, giving exaggerated danger signals that some savage and remorseless enemy was on his tail.

One morning the puppies were surprised by the Master strolling into the orchard, leading a huge creature of their own kind. None of them guessed that this queen-like animal was Tara, their mother, while she gave no indication that these were her children. After a minute or two of embarrassed watchfulness, Finn approached Tara bravely, his tail hanging limply as he sniffed warily at her legs. Discovering that this great hound meant them no harm, he soon adopted an air of familiarity that gave heart to his brothers and sister, who were soon sniffing respectfully at Tara's legs. For a moment the mother of heroes pretended this attention was of no interest to her but, once the Master tactfully turned his back, she filled the pups with surprise and delight by first stretching cat-like and then springing around the youngsters. When the Master turned back, the five of them were frolicking wildly with the impudent Finn growling theatrically, and leaping at the loose skin round her throat, eyes staring and jaws gaping.

From then on Tara spent most of her days in the orchard. When she was tired of playing she'd stretch out under the oak tree, letting it be known that she wasn't to be disturbed. If this didn't work she'd astound the pups by clearing the gate and retiring to the peace of the Master's den for an hour or so.

On one occasion she opened a whole new way of life for the pups. At the top end of the orchard, nearest the Downs, were a number of rabbit warrens. Tara and the pups had wandered that way and had surprised an unwary rabbit that had let the dogs get between him and his warren. Too late the rabbit stopped his nibbling and headed for safety. Tara bounded forward and cut off his retreat. Wheeling in the opposite direction, the rabbit flew towards a gap in the fence. Tara followed like the wind with the four pups yapping in pursuit. Halfway across the orchard, Tara overtook the rabbit, her great jaws closing round its back and fatally crushing the spinal column. Finn arrived on the scene in a frenzy of excitement. Tara drew back loftily but Finn sprang on the dead body, snarling and snapping, whirling it round and round his head until his throat was half choked with fur. Then the other pups joined in, grabbing and tugging at whatever they could get their teeth into. The noise they made attracted the Master and the pups saw nothing more of their victim.

Even so, the experience had brought a new interest into Finn's life and much of his time was now spent near the rabbit warrens. Many glorious chases followed but, as yet, he simply didn't have the speed to catch them, nor the power in his jaws to make the kill. Nevertheless, he found enormous joy in stalking, hunting and lying in wait.

On one mellow September afternoon, while busily tearing the canvas from a hammock chair, the four pups looked up and saw the Master and Mistress and a stately white-haired lady who fondled Tara's beautiful head as they walked. The lady, who had brought Tara and the Master back together again, was staying with friends in Sussex and had been invited to meet Tara's family.

'You haven't found homes for any of the puppies yet?' she asked.

'Oh, no. I wanted to wait until you had a chance of making your choice,' the Master replied. 'It would be such a small return for your help, but I would like you to have one of the family.'

The three settled down to inspect the pups at leisure.

'That grey is Finn. We weighed him yesterday and he's four kilograms heavier than the nearest of the others – and they're as big as I've seen before. Finn will be a champion one day and will do you credit if you chose him.'

The visitor was clearly moved. She guessed how much pride the Master had centred on Finn.

'Finn is quite splendid, there's no doubt. But to be honest I'd rather have a female. That way I'd feel I *also* had a future mother of heroes.'

The Master felt an undeniable thrill at the prospect of keeping Finn. He'd felt sure that Finn would be chosen and was quite prepared to make the sacrifice if necessary. Now though, he had the means of repaying his debt and keeping Finn. Still, honesty impelled him to point out that the Yorkshire lady might never have the chance again of such a hound. The lady stuck to her preference and so it was decided.

A week later a second visitor came, this time from Somerset. Despite spending half an hour trying to persuade the Master to let him have Finn, he left with the fawn whelp in his travelling hamper.

'I still think it's a mistake not to accept my offer for the grey,' the breeder insisted as he left.

As autumn advanced, Finn and his remaining sister lived more like grown hounds, with the privileges of grown-ups. They learned to enter the den with Tara and behave with discretion. They never saw a whip, but the Master's sharp voice stopped them in their tracks when tempted to chew a newspaper or rip fabrics. From Tara they learned the dignity and deportment that becomes a Wolfhound.

Towards the end of November their meals were reduced from four to three, and they were given green leather collars with the Master's name inscribed on brass. These were for outside use only and with them came lessons in leading, which required a good deal of patience on the Mistress' part.

As a rule, the Master took Tara and the youngsters out on the Downs early in the morning. It was on one such walk that Finn tasted the joy and pride of his first kill, some time in his sixth month. He and Tara had started after a rabbit which had scurried from behind a hillock not more than ten paces from them. Wheeling from under Tara's nose the rabbit was bound to cross Finn's path. His heart swelled and his jaws gripped hot desire as he galloped. Just as Tara had shown them, Finn's jaws seized his prey a little behind the shoulders. Although he still didn't have the power to kill instantly, he shook the rabbit so vigorously that it was nevertheless dead when Tara arrived. After a brief inspection Tara sat on her haunches, indicating that she had no intention of interfering with Finn's trophy. As for Finn, he was unsure what to do. The rabbit was killed with enough thoroughness for six rabbits. Obscure instincts flitted through Finn's mind as he jerkily licked and then withdrew from his kill. In the main his instinct said 'tear and kill.' On the other hand, he wasn't hungry. The Master always ensured that they had a few titbits to discourage them from picking up anything less desirable. It was a long time since his kind had killed for food. Certainly, no dog could have taken the rabbit from Finn, but when the Master ordered him to drop it he obeyed.

In that quiet corner of Sussex it was rare for Wolfhounds to meet other dogs. When they did, it was a matter of course for them to treat the others as lesser creatures. They never made advances, but patiently allowed strangers to sniff around them as they stood aloof. Even at that young age they had enormous dignity. The thought of snapping at dog or human never occurred to them. Certainly, some animals were there to chase but it never occurred to Finn that there might be anything to fear or hate.

5

The ordeal of the ring

Finn's first winter was a mild one. It passed without his noticing anything remarkable about the climate. But spring entered his veins and new vitality and growth surged through his lusty young body. Long, slow trots behind a bicycle hardened Finn's feet without overstraining his legs.

On the morning of his first birthday, Finn, with his sister Kathleen, Tara and the Master, walked down to the railway station to be weighed. He was exactly fifty-four kilograms, some twelve kilograms more than his sister and only six kilograms less than Tara. From the ground to his shoulder he measured eighty-nine centimetres. Yet, Finn still wouldn't be fully grown until late in his second year.

Three months of Downland summer saw the hunting of innumerable rabbits, out-of-door days some fifteen hours long and a steady increase in road work, fortified by three good meals a day.

In October, the Master introduced a new game, vaguely amusing but one which didn't seem to have much point. A ring of sticks was marked out in the orchard in which the Mistress would act as director of ceremonies. With the help of a maid or local boy, Tara, Finn and Kathleen would be led round and round the ring by the Master, while the Mistress of the Kennels looked on. Resentful of the lead, Finn at first pulled to the side. Always in front of him though, he had the graceful example of his mother, who simply kept the lead gently tight as she marched round with her head held well up and her tail hanging in a graceful curve. Gradually it dawned on Finn that this walk was a matter of pride and he was being judged. By the end of the week he could stride out as elegantly as Tara or bound forward with the spring of elastic, all at the touch of his Master's hand. When asked, he could stand erect with one paw on the Master's finger held shoulder high. Alternatively, he could stand at attention with feet spread evenly and tail curved correctly. The ease with which he could be praised by the Master for such simple actions amused Finn who tended to forget the hours of practice.

Then came the October morning when, instead of their scamper across the Downs, Finn and Kathleen were treated to an elaborate grooming. An air of impending excitement filled the room. Tara became even more restless at the sight of two new, nickel chains with unusual little tin medals attached. Tara watched wistfully as they filed out on to the road. She returned to the den and lay with her muzzle on the Master's slippers.

At the station Finn weighed in at sixty-three kilograms. 'We have to remember, of course, that Finn's development is probably several months ahead of other hounds,' said the Master, 'but it's still pretty good at that.'

A train roared into the station causing Finn and his sister to lower their tails and pull away. Once inside the carriage their chains were removed, allowing Finn to look through the window with his nose pressed against the glass. When the train started with a jerk, the sensation of travel upset Finn. It seemed as though the ground was being snatched from under him. He barked loudly as trees and houses flashed by alarmingly, almost seeming to brush his nose on the window. The Mistress laughed and patted his head reassuringly. Finn didn't bark again for he was both puzzled and interested by the things he saw.

In due course, the chains were attached once more. By now, Finn had become quite blasé about travelling, as well as a little weary. From the train the hounds were led through a crush of people – more than they thought existed in the whole world. Some of these people were also leading dogs on chains and Finn became very self-conscious, rather like a country cousin who found himself surrounded by London's fashionable folk.

New experiences crowded in thick and fast. After pressing through the throng, Finn and Kathleen came face-to-face with the first flight of stairs they'd ever seen. True, each hound had a comforting hand guiding them along, but the stairs were still a shock. At first glance they seemed to call for small leaps and bounds but climbing this way invariably brought their noses into contact with strangers; an undignified experience implying familiarity, which Finn didn't want.

Eventually, the stairs came to an end, followed by a long stretch of open road. Finally, after being allowed to run for a while in a quiet street, the hounds were led into a large building, containing countless humans and all the dogs in the world, all talking incoherently together. In fact there were thousands of dogs at Crystal Palace that day, the opening session of the Kennel Club Show – the biggest event of the year.

It's hard to imagine how much of an ordeal the show must have been for Finn and Kathleen to face. They were led down the length of this enormous building between rows of yapping terriers of every size, to a spot where thirty or forty other Wolfhounds were waiting. Until that day, neither of them had seen more than a handful of dogs. Here, the noise of barking, the variety and pungency of the smells and the sheer variety of breeds were at first overpowering. Finn and Kathleen surveyed their surroundings with lowered tails, darting eyes and raised hackles. But the pride and self-confidence which comes from strength soon came to Finn's aid; and by the time they reached their own bench his tail and head were carried high, even though his heart was far from comfortable.

Although the benches were continuous, the space allotted for each dog was divided by strong iron netting, and their chains were securely attached to the back of the bench. Finn had his sister to his right and (though he didn't know

35

it) his father – the Champion Dermot Asthore – to his left. Old Dermot Asthore took no more notice of Finn than the rest of the show. He was extremely bored and was dreading the three days of the event.

The Mistress of the Kennels sat on a little camp stool between Finn and Kathleen. The Master flitted to and fro chatting to people he knew, but never straying too far away from his hounds. In his hand was a yellow book giving him details of every dog at the show. The Mistress studied her own copy. If Finn could have read he'd have seen she was busy studying the Wolfhound section, which was divided into three sections – Open, Limit and Novice.

It was obvious that competition would be stiff. In the Open section there were several champions and prize winners of high repute. The other sections also had their fair share of well-fancied hounds. Finn and Kathleen were not only in the Junior section for both sexes under the age of eighteen months, but had also been boldly entered in every other division for which they were eligible. Some of the older breeders, who hadn't seen them, smiled at the enthusiasm which put fifteen-month-old youngsters in the Open class against champions with considerable reputations.

Now and then, exhibitors would pause, look at the pair of them and remark on their age. Looking up the details they would nod knowledgeably as they read of Dermot the sire and Tara the dam. Finn had the notion that these men were as knowledgeable as the Master and would have obeyed them readily.

By the time Finn had outgrown the novelty of his surroundings and had decided on a sleep, the Master returned in something of a rush. Chains were unsnapped and Finn and his sister were taken down from the bench. A number of other Wolfhounds did the same and all were led towards a square, fenced-in judging enclosure. The dog section was about to be judged, and Kathleen was brought along to keep her settled. The Master was leading Finn.

Before entering the ring, he stroked the dog's eyebrows and beard.

Accompanied by a busy steward, the judge stood in the centre of the ring, a sheaf of papers in his hand. No man living cóuld claim to know more about Wolfhounds than this white-haired old gentleman.

'Move them round please,' he said quietly, 'as freely as possible.'

Finn was the only hound under two and a half years, a child amongst acknowledged leaders and chieftains. His legs were more angular and he carried less flesh than the others. In the dog world they had 'furnished' while Finn had not. The Mistress, from her position outside the ring, noticed all these things and wondered about their over-enthusiasm of entering Finn in such company.

'Finn boy!' she whispered as he walked by. Instantly the youngster's ears picked up and his fine neck curved superbly as he looked round. The Master then bent down close, whispering those nonsense sounds Finn associated with events such as rabbit hunting and racing on the Downs.

'Chu, chu, chu-u-u, Finn,' he crooned, as he had while walking Finn round the temporary ring in the orchard. Thus it was that Finn realised he was on display and being judged against others of his kind. From that moment he showed the best in him to show. With the air of a king, he paraded round the ring as proud as any of his warrior ancestors.

When they next neared the judge, the Master touched Finn's side, the sign for him to tower on his hind legs to his full height, way above a man's head.

'Down Finn, down!' the Master pretended to rebuke but Finn recognised the tone and knew all was well. The judge chewed on his pencil and from time to time, with a nod or a word of thanks, asked one of the exhibitors to leave the ring.

It was on the fifth circuit that the judge nodded towards the Master with a few muttered words. The Master's face fell and downheartedly, he began walking away. The steward ran up to him fussily and explained that he wasn't to withdraw but to stand in a corner with the likes of Dermot Asthore. A moment later, the ring was clear except for three hounds and Finn.

Now came the most searching of inspections, drawn up in a row before the judge. Teeth, eyes, claws, all were minutely examined by the man who had studied these matters for fifty years. Muscles and joints were felt in a way any self-respecting hound would resent. Then the four walked round once more in single file, and then singly, to and fro, to and fro. Finally, the height to their shoulders was measured. The judge carried this out four times with Finn, each time squinting at his tape.

'Eighty-nine and a half centimetres. I must say, this is the largest fifteen-month-old I've ever seen. Quite remarkable, sir.'

Cormac's master was told to stand aside and a murmur went round the spectators that here was the winner. Munster was the next to step aside, leaving only Dermot and Finn. The crowd wondered who would get third place, the celebrated champion or the new comer.

At last the judge drew back saying: 'Thank you, that will be all.'

The crowd surged round the notice-board. Excitement was high, for this was the most important Wolfhound class in the show. The Master shot a smile to the Mistress and fondled Finn's ears before pressing forward to see the results.

1st	No. 247
2nd	No. 248
3rd	No. 261
VHC	No. 256
HC	No. 259

Not daring to be certain, the Master drew out the little medal on Finn's collar and read the number again: 247.

Finn had been declared winner in the Open Class for Irish Wolfhounds in the show. His sire, Dermot had come second and Munster third.

On hearing the news, the Mistress of the Kennels flung her arms round Finn's neck while Finn nosed poor Kathleen who had been temporarily forgotten.

'You great, beautiful Finn. Do you realise you've come first? You've beaten all the champions,' she said.

Finn nuzzled her shoulder and wondered why something so obvious had ever been in any doubt. Nevertheless, it was a great triumph, the greatest that had ever fallen to a breeder, as some of the competitors who came to congratulate him pointed out.

'For a fifteen-month novice, against two champions,' they said, 'wonderful!'

'He's the tallest now,' said the judge, lingering to pass his hand over Finn's shoulder. 'He'll be the biggest and finest I've handled and I've seen most of them.'

In the Limit and Novice Finn was awarded first place as a matter of course. There was nothing there to beat him. In the bitches section, Kathleen also did extremely well: third in the Open, second in the Limit and first place Novice.

Finn finally had to be judged against the winner in the Open class for bitches, to see who would win the Challenge Shield for best Irish Wolfhound. The white-haired judge agonised for a long time over his decision. The female was Lady Iseult of Leinster, one of the most beautiful hounds her sex had ever seen and recognised world-wide. Technically it was difficult to find fault with her except, perhaps, the hock section of her legs was a little straight. Finn's, on the other hand, were curved like an Arabian stallion's, springy like a cat. The judge compared the two of them side by side many times in every possible way he could. Finally, he asked if they could both be run, as quickly as possible, while being led.

Still the conscientious old man wasn't satisfied. He called for a hurdle to be brought in and Lady Iseult was invited to jump over. She did so gracefully and quietly returned to her master. Then Finn was unchained and the Mistress called him from the far side of the ring. He bounded forward with the elasticity of a cat, clearing the hurdle by a good two feet.

The judge stroked his beard, laid a hand on the two dogs and declared:

'The young dog has it. He's the finest hound I've ever seen!'

6

Revelations

It's the custom at dog shows for the winner to receive coloured cards, denoting the positions they've reached. At this show, first place was blue, second red and third yellow.

So when Finn returned to his place on the bench, he sat beneath a dome of blue cards as well as ribbons signifying his victory in the Challenge Shield. He also had a number of special prizes including a two guinea prize donated by a famous Irish sportsman for the biggest Wolfhound in the Show.

His many trophies created much attention for him, even amongst the majority of visitors who didn't appreciate his technical claims to fame. There was always a group of admirers around him, begging the Master to take him down from the bench so they could see him better. Then there were the men from the newspapers with their notebooks and cameras and even the dealers with their fat cheque-books.

That evening, Finn received more coverage in the papers than any human. Although he couldn't read, Finn was more conscious of his fame than you might suppose. He was aware that he'd greatly pleased the Master and Mistress, making him both happy and proud.

It was ten o'clock at night when they finally left the Show. Apart from their activity in the ring, Finn and Kathleen had received very little exercise and were now thoroughly tired of the attention and noise. The Mistress had already returned to Tara, but the two hounds were staying in lodgings close to Crystal Palace. They didn't yet realise that one of the penalties of fame was that the dogs were obliged to remain at the show for two more days.

On the evening of the second day, while the Master was talking to someone a little distance away, the young hounds were visited by a man who showed extreme interest in them. His appearance reminded Finn of a gamekeeper he knew in Sussex, and by his various smells it was clear he spent much time with dogs. The man looked up Finn's ancestry in the show catalogue and then fondled him for several minutes. Before turning away, this friendly man passed Finn a piece of meat from a paper bag in his pocket. Of all the meat he'd eaten, this had the most fascinating and exciting smell of all. On the final afternoon, the man returned. Finn welcomed him warmly with his nose and paw, obviously looking for more of the meat. The man chuckled and rubbed Finn's ears affectionately for several minutes. Before leaving he presented Finn with another piece of the meat with the fascinating smell.

By paying a small fee, the Master was able to take Finn and Kathleen away from the show early. A few hours later, all three were being welcomed by the Mistress of the Kennels and Tara. The three hounds dined sumptuously while the Master and Mistress relived their triumphs in the show ring. Afterwards, they were allowed out for a romp in the orchard before going to bed.

Immediately Tara reached the orchard she gave a loud 'Who's there' bark. Normally the Master would have investigated. Perhaps it was because he was tired or chatting – who knows – but he paid no attention. On the other hand, to his delight Finn found the stranger he'd met at the show standing by the gate. Tara eyed him haughtily, as one does with someone unknown. But Finn, remembering the tasty meat the man specialised in, stood up on the gate and lolled his tongue in friendly greeting. The man rewarded him enticingly with a tasty piece of meat and rubbed the youngster's ears in the coaxing way he had. Then he stepped back several paces and produced a larger chunk.

'Here boy. Here Finn. Jump boy!' The gate was a metre and a half and the seductive smell of meat floated just beyond it in the still night air. Taking a short run, Finn cleared the gate easily. While feeding Finn his prize the man slipped a swivel on to the ring of his collar and attached a strong leather lead. The man moved off slowly, with another piece of meat in his hand. Finn followed willingly enough and by the time he'd finished chewing he was a hundred metres away. Looking back, a vaguely uncomfortable thrill passed through his body. He stopped and wondered if he should return to Tara and Kathleen. If the stranger had tried to force him then it would have spelt trouble. Instead he rubbed Finn's ears and brought out another tasty piece of meat. Holding it out once more he moved off, and Finn forgot his doubts. After all, he thought, this is probably another novelty of the show.

While he was eating, the man slipped another collar round his neck, removing the green one. He began to trot, which pleased Finn more. They travelled for many kilometres through the still October night, the man breathing easily. Something made Finn stop suddenly and he realised that this new collar was totally different to any he'd experienced so far. If you pulled hard it tightened round your neck cutting off your breath. The only thing to do was go in the direction the lead was pulling and immediately the pressure relaxed. Evidently, it was a device which needed obeying.

Eventually they reached a little town and in the yard of an inn, they met a second man. 'I'll walk on. You follow in the cart,' the stranger instructed, 'and don't stop till you're clear of the village.'

Once more Finn was led along, through the streets and out into the countryside. By this time he was beginning to think his walk had gone on long enough. No more aromatic meat came his way. He thought he'd like to turn now and go home.

Accordingly, Finn asked to stop. Finding the man took no notice, Finn tried again, snorting urgently down his nose. Again he was ignored, annoying Finn who planted his feet and stopped dead. The slip-collar pressed painfully on his throat but Finn was determined to return home. The man gave a powerful tug on the lead, forcing Finn's tongue from his mouth.

'Come on you brute!' growled the man, giving another vicious jerk on the lead. He stepped to the side and kicked Finn as hard as he could on his hind quarters. That was the first real blow Finn had ever received, and it taught him a lot. It had never occurred to him that the stranger could be anything other than friendly. And it hurt.

Turning the way they'd come, Finn plunged forward with such strength he almost pulled the lead from the man's hand. As it was, the sudden jerk of the slip-collar throttled Finn, pulling him off his feet and on to his back. Two more vicious kicks landed in his ribs and Finn was thankful to slacken the lead and draw breath.

Just then the lights of a cart appeared from the direction of the village.

'That you Bill? Come on let's get this beast in the back.'

Another savage yank and a brutal kick to the ribs bewildered Finn. Finn leapt sideways, moving his great body out of the way. This sudden movement startled the horse, who shied violently, swerving the cart into the hedge; a cracking sound betraying the breaking of a shaft.

This put the finishing touches to the man's vicious temper. He cursed endlessly and his accomplice tried to repair the damage with cord and a couple of sticks. With every curse there was a kick or a blow or a savage jerk on the torturous chain. Finn could have killed the man with ease but so far the idea of biting him had never occurred to him.

The man instinctively knew this and it put an edge on his cruelty. He had no real wish to hurt the hound, in fact, exactly the opposite as Finn meant considerable money to him. But things were going wrong and the cause – a sensitive living creature – was tethered and helpless beside him.

Once the shaft was mended, the tail-board was dropped and with a savage kick Finn was urged on to the cart.

'Get up you brute.' Another kick and a yank. Poor Finn tried to squirm forward under the cart to escape the beating but was dragged backwards, choking.

The driver was used to this anger and said nothing. But he hated to see money go to waste and so lifted Finn's front paws on to the cart.

'My oath, but he's a tidy weight. Up you go, my bully boy.'

And up Finn went, spurred on by another boot scraping the skin off his hock. The big man knelt on Finn while his lead was tied closely to a bracket on the cart.

The memory of that journey burned into Finn's memory and forever more his attitude towards men changed. Every bone ached and his skin was broken in several places. He was desperately thirsty and his muzzle was held down tightly to the grimy floorboards in the cart. For one who had never even received a severe scolding, that night was a terrible ordeal.

At last, though, the journey came to an end.

'Thank Gawd, 'ere's 'orley,' said the driver as the cart came to a stop in a walled-in yard. The horse was stabled and the man from the show dropped the tail-gate, dragging Finn off so that he fell to the ground with a thud. Cramped and sore beyond belief, Finn staggered to his feet before being dragged into an evil-smelling room about four feet square. Horrible smells rose from the filthy earthen floor. There was no drainage or ventilation except a few holes in the door which was slammed and locked behind the youngster.

'What about a drink for 'im?' asked the driver.

'A drink be blowed! Let 'im wait. I can't tell you 'ow glad I am that night's work is over. If I don't make fifty quid out of this I'll want to know why. Big ugly brute. Strong as a mule 'e is. *I'd* want to be paid for keeping the likes of 'im. Still the American gent's red 'ot to get 'is 'ands on 'im. Biggest ever bred they tell me.'

Their voices were a misery to poor Finn, shivering and aching in his cell. His sensitive nose wrinkled in horror and disgust. How could they torture him this way without water? This was a sad plight for the hero of the Kennel Club Show.

7

Finn walks alone

For a long while after the men left, Finn remained standing, taking up as small a space as possible. His careful rearing worked against him now. Until this night he had never been without water, nor smelled anything quite so horrible as this cell. Finn could hardly bring himself to move. He shivered by the door, his nose breathing through a crack by the hinge.

Gradually, thoughts of Tara and Kathleen entered his mind, as did the sweet cleanliness and freedom of his home on the Downs. But instead of comforting him, they seemed to add to his loneliness and the pains of his aching body. Unable to bear them any longer, Finn turned to the centre of his prison cell. Avoiding contact with the walls and loathing every second, Finn scraped a hollow with his feet. It was about the size of a wash basin and just large enough for him to sit on his haunches.

He was suddenly overcome with the need to tell Tara and the Master of his sorry plight. So, sitting in the one clean spot available, he pointed his long muzzle towards the stars he couldn't see and opened his jaws wide. Finn howled in true Irish Wolfhound tradition; a sound which seemed to find its way out from the very centre of his grieving heart. Winding slowly through his lungs and throat it reached the air with the effect of a steamship's siren. It is a sound which carries a very long way and one difficult to ignore.

Finn was rumbling out his sixth howl when the door burst in and his captor appeared armed with a lamp and heavy stick. Finn was so new to the ways of unfriendly humans that he thought his howls had brought him release. The images of cool drinking water, a meal and a clean bed flitted briefly across his mind. If he hadn't been so loath to touch the walls, his tail would even have wagged. Instead the man's stick crashed down on his nose – the most delicate and sensitive spot on his body. The blow was hideously painful and unexpected. It robbed Finn of sight, sense and self-respect. In just a few seconds, the proudest of princes had been turned into a shuddering, cringing object, cowering in the corner of a filthy shed.

The man was both furious and afraid. Already, a number of bedroom windows had been raised, and he wanted to avoid unnecessary questions. He set about quieting Finn. Closing the door behind him he rained blows down on the dog until his arm ached and Finn's cries subsided. Satisfied with his work, the man threw the stick in Finn's face, leaving him whimpering in paralysed shame with one rib broken.

For a long time Finn felt nothing but fear, pain and misery. Gently, he began to lick some of his wounds until he fell asleep, exhausted. When he awoke, most of his pains still remained but fear had given way to a determination to escape from this cruel man. So far, nothing in his short life had equipped him for this kind of ordeal. All he had to draw on was instinct. He was fully aware that he must take the first chance he had of getting away.

For the first time, Finn examined his cell carefully. He used his sense of smell and touch as there was precious little light. His nose was sore from the blows but he overcame this, as well as the smell, only to find that there was nothing here to help him. Three sides were brick and the fourth was the door which offered no edge or corner for him to attack with his teeth. There was nothing to do but wait, his tongue lolling out in excruciating thirst. Every hour strengthened his determination and taught him something of patience and caution.

Presently, Finn heard heavy footsteps in the yard. His muscles tightened for action. The door opened and his tormentor stood there with stick and chain in hand.

'Come 'ere!' said the man. Finn came, unexpectedly low and hard, straight through his legs and into the yard. The man was not worried, the yard was quite secure. Having slept well he was in a good mood. Still, there was no time to waste. He had to groom Finn before the buyer came. Bending on one knee, he tried to sound friendly and coax Finn to him.

'Here, then, good dog. Come on, Finn boy.'

Instinct gave Finn the edge over the man. A swift inspection had told him it was impossible to escape from the yard. He stood quietly, half a dozen steps from his gaoler, every muscle ready for action. The man moved forward with hand outstretched. Finn's hackles rose as he stepped back. They moved round the yard this way perhaps six times, keeping a constant distance between the two of them.

It was here that the man's intelligence failed him. He was expecting the rich American who would have his reward for stealing Finn to arrive any minute; he had to get his hands on the dog. Frustrated by their tour of the yard he threw the chain at Finn angrily and, cursing, went indoors to work out another plan.

Finn lightly sidestepped the missile and gave an angry bark. While the man was away, Finn inspected the gate. It wobbled and rattled encouragingly but remained solidly shut even when he stood his full weight against it.

The man reappeared with some of his tasty meat. Finn, though, had learned much in the last twelve hours. He took the centre of the yard and ignored the man's friendly overtures. The man cursed Finn who still refused to trust him. He tried tossing the meat to Finn's feet, but Finn resisted the temptation. If the man had been wiser, he'd have realised that water might have been more attractive to Finn at that moment.

Running out of ideas the man charged at Finn, stick held high. Now and then he got a blow to land as Finn ducked and weaved in the narrow space. This chasing was bad for Finn. It gnawed at everything he held dear. It wasn't punishment such as he'd received the night before, however unreasonable that might have been. Instead, it was sheer savagery. The savagery of a running fight during which he might hurt occasionally but could not conquer.

The man was becoming exhausted and in another moment or two would have probably given up his senseless pursuit. But just then, the gate opened and the driver appeared. In an instant, Finn dived for the opening. The driver's legs were bowled aside and he stumbled to the ground, an oath on his lips. Finn reached the open road. Behind him he heard hurried scrambling and a good deal of breathless whistling and calling. Then he heard no more from his place of captivity for he was already near the limits of town and galloping hard for the open country, over the road he'd travelled the previous night.

For five kilometres Finn galloped, his heart swelling with the joy of his freedom. Then, gradually, his pace slowed, first to a canter and then to a trot. The sight of a wayside pool brought him to a standstill. After a quick look over his shoulder, Finn waded into the refreshing water and drank till he could drink no more. He emerged from the water, his muzzle dripping and his bruises aching. He lay down on the grass and licked those wounds within reach, conscious of the sharp pain of his broken rib. Gaining confidence, the young hound stretched out and began to doze.

Presently, a cart from the town approached carrying two extremely angry men. Both wanted their money while the man from the show wanted Finn's hide. His heavy mouth twitched as he thought how he'd tie up the dog and beat it senseless.

'I'm jiggered if that aint 'im waiting for us!' exclaimed the driver.

His mate was out of the cart in a second. Meat in hand and with a whining greeting, he headed for Finn. But Finn had heard the cart and had sprung to his feet. On seeing his enemy, he was off like a wolf down the empty road. Another lesson had been learned; no more would he rest by the wayside.

After three kilometres of galloping at thirty-five kilometres an hour, Finn slowed to a loping pace that would have matched anything on the road except a car. Eventually, though, the pain in his side forced him to stop. With a stab like a knife, Finn cleared a field-gate and crept along a hedge before curling up, half-buried, in the safety of dry hay and straw. Desperate for rest, sleep came quickly. The young hound whimpered occasionally and once or twice his body shook to the sound of growling barks. Finn drove his muzzle deeper into the dry hay under his hocks, and allowed sleep to do its healing.

Finn awoke to the sight of the setting sun. All round him was the silence of the twilight. He yawned cavernously and stretched his huge frame, but the sharp pain in his side stopped him short. Slowly, Finn rose and walked into the darkening twilight. Before he'd got far, a rabbit started up from behind a bush, scurrying for its life towards the hedge. The distance was too great and within two metres of safety Finn snapped its backbone. Though Finn had killed many rabbits, until then he had never eaten one. Now, the instinct for survival drove Finn to eat the unfortunate creature, giving him yet another new experience.

After his meal, Finn strolled on till he found a gap in the hedge. For a kilometre or two, he trotted along the road before turning into a grassy lane. Eventually, Finn came to three hay stacks. His side ached and he was disappointed not to have found any sign of his home. Finn missed his friends. He sat on his haunches and once more turned his head to the stars and howled. He howled this way for five minutes before scratching and burrowing up in a curl in one of the ricks.

Long before the dew had dried Finn set out to do something he'd never done before: to hunt and kill an animal for food. He very nearly caught an unwary partridge. In the end, his menu was the same as the previous night. As he eyed the rabbit's still warm and furry remains, Finn felt that life wasn't so bad after all.

Towards midday, Finn lounged into a village which he

didn't like at all. It reminded him too much of the enemies on his trail. He hurried on and towards the end of the village he passed a pretty, creeper-covered cottage. A policeman leaving the cottage noticed Finn and called him:

'Here, boy! Here, good dog.'

But Finn lengthened his stride and broke into a gallop. He was no longer the trustful Finn of a week ago. The constable watched Finn's disappearing body.

'He must be the dog that's wanted, right enough. Regular monster he is. In fact, I'd just as soon he was found somewhere else. I reckon my missus would have a fit. It don't seem right having dogs that size.'

Half an hour later Finn found, to his delight, that he'd left the houses and roads behind and was on the familiar chalky hills of the Sussex Downs. The great, blunt hills and the close-cropped springy turf brought a rush of home-feeling to Finn's heart. With misty eyes, he sat down and gave two or three long-drawn-out howls as an expression of melancholy. But Finn's nose told him he'd never been on this part of the Downs before.

Towards evening he ran down and killed another rabbit, leaving half for a weasel following in his tracks. Something, perhaps the fact that his day had not been exhausting, prevented him from curling up and sleeping. The night was clear and fine, and the many strange wild life noises enticed him on.

Later on, too much freedom lost its allure and he longed to be with his family. It was about this time that Finn found himself on a narrow, white sheep-walk which seemed more homely than any he'd crossed that evening. Gradually, the chalky track deepened and widened, becoming a path sunk into the hillside to a depth of five metres or so. It ended in a five-bar gate, which Finn leaped over with a strange feeling of exultation. Something rose in his throat; his eyes became misty and his nose dropped eagerly to the ground. Whimpering softly he began to run, his tail swaying from side to side.

Two minutes later, Finn came to a white gate. It led

to a shrub-sheltered garden in front of a small, low rambling house. He leaped over the gate and turned sharply to the right. His way was blocked by a high door which he couldn't possibly climb or jump. He sat on his haunches and howled steadily for one and a half minutes, only stopping when the door opened and a man clad in pyjamas rushed out into the garden.

Finn had grown to avoid men, but this time he rose on his hind legs to give a greeting, and he could hardly be persuaded to lower his paws as the Master removed his comforting arms from the Wolfhound's shoulders. Three minutes later, Finn was joined by the Mistress of the Kennels.

8

The heart of Tara

The Mistress held on to one of Finn's paws as though she was afraid he'd be spirited away. His 'fatted calf' came in the form of sardines on toast intended for the Master's breakfast, and a dish of warm milk. Finn felt the occasion was special and polished them off more from politeness than from hunger. The Master quickly spotted the slip collar and removed it.

'Well, that puts paid to the theory that Finn wandered off,' he said. 'If the police know their business this ought to help.'

He turned to Finn again. 'You didn't know there was a £25 reward, did you? I'd have made it £50 in a day or so, although heaven knows, our bank balance says we should sell you rather than spend more on you.'

As he spoke, the Master examined Finn carefully, parting his thick hair to see the places where the skin was broken and pressing his fingers along the lines of bones and muscles. When Finn winced from the pain in his ribs, the Master cursed under his breath.

'There's a rib broken here,' he said to the Mistress. 'When the post office opens tomorrow, we must wire the vet. Thieving's bad enough, but this . . . Poor Finn's been handled more roughly than an understanding man would handle a tiger. Look at his face and into his eyes. He's even watchful of me. Well, my old son, without doubt you've said goodbye to puppyhood. I'll bet he's learned more in these three days than in the rest of his life. Watch his eyes as I raise my hand.'

The Master jerked his hand upwards and they could see a look in his eyes they'd never seen in Tara or Kathleen. Neither of them had had to pit their wits against humans. They'd never been clubbed or seen the ugly side of human nature. Wave your arms in front of them and one would ignore you while the other would think it was some new game.

It may be, of course, that Finn's experiences made him better equipped to face the world, but the Master sighed deeply for the loss of utter trustfulness.

Still, Finn was back and this went a long way towards countering the anger the Master felt; especially after their triumphs at the show. The seven prize cards were pinned above Tara's great bed, but they seemed a mockery in Finn's absence. When the Master and Mistress finally said goodnight to Finn, they made sure the coach house was carefully padlocked.

In less than a month, physically, Finn was as good as new. His ribs were sound and all his wounds had healed, although a light scar remained on his muzzle where the man's stick had bitten into the bone. If it had been nine months earlier, it might have been a different story, for setbacks in puppyhood are hard to make up. But Finn had the physical foundation for his life to go on without interruption.

The winter weather turned severe and his recovery continued in ideal conditions. Finn breathed England's heartiest air, fed well and regularly, and exercised daily. When summer came, he was weighed on his second birthday at sixty-seven and a half kilograms, while measuring ninety-one and a half centimetres at the shoulder.

Although it's the custom to measure Wolfhounds in this way, you should remember that his head would be another thirty centimetres higher. When standing on all fours, Finn could rest his nose on a window-ledge more than a metre high. His eyes, shaggy brows and beard were as dark as night while the rest of him, except for a few stray dark hairs, were steely-grey just like the wolves who lived in the north.

It was a colour that suggested ghostly speed and enduring strength. His legs were as straight as gun barrels; his feet hard, round and rather cat-like except his nails were like chisels. By contrast, his hind legs were finely curved, with rolls of swelling muscle on his upper thighs. His chest was deep, like an Arab stallion, while his long, arching neck bulged with muscles. It was difficult to say he'd grown much since his fifteenth month and yet he'd filled out and was a much bigger and stronger dog. He might put on a few more kilograms, but he was now at his peak; a superb specimen of pure breeding and perfect rearing.

For some six months, Finn's only canine companion had been Tara. He had not seen Kathleen's departure and for some days was puzzled by her absence. He had stood by the gate and growled fiercely, his fur almost standing on end thinking perhaps the thief had returned. In fact, he needn't have worried; Kathleen had gone to a good home. Her owner had paid one hundred guineas and wouldn't sell her for ten times that amount. But of course there was no way of telling Finn these things. Finn understood most of what the Master told him but would never understand the financial problems that had forced the Master to sell Kathleen.

But Kathleen's sale was by no means the end of his difficulties. At the heart of the trouble was the Master's inability to earn much money in the country, but that was where he wanted to live. So it was that the Master began to spend a good deal of time away from the house. Tara was used to spending much of her day in the den, her feet on the Master's slippers. Finn was completely different. While Tara lay dreaming at home, he loved nothing better than to be chasing alongside the Mistress as she rode her bicycle. The Mistress liked to think that her fifteen kilometre ride tired Finn out, but she never saw the dozen other kilometres which Finn covered alone on his hunting trips. The weasels, stoats and rabbits could have told the Mistress why he did not always clear his plate each night. He was safe enough on these solo trips too, for he had only angry growls for men of his kidnapper's ilk.

In some ways, Finn suffered through the Master's absence, and so did the rabbits. But in other ways it made him a harder, more wily hunter than he might otherwise have become.

One day in late summer, something happened which Finn never forgot. The Master had been away for three weeks and Tara missed him sadly. In the evenings, the bitch would whimper quietly to the slippers the Mistress never thought to remove. Now, with the hint of autumn in the evening, Finn lay beside Tara in the den, dreaming of an area of the Downs he intended to hunt. Outside on the gravel came the sound of footsteps. Tara's nose quivered and with one bound she was outside the den.

'Tara! Here girl!' The Master stood by the open gate. Finn saw his mother fly through the air like an arrow from a bow. Six great bounds she gave while Finn made twenty. Then Tara stopped suddenly. With a strange moaning cry, she staggered and fell sideways as the Master ran to her side. Her head was resting against his knee and with glazed eyes turned for a last glimpse of the face she loved, Tara died.

Finn was sniffing at his mother's back. He didn't understand what had happened, but he knew instinctively that great sadness was in the air and that his beautiful mother was the victim.

The shock to the Master was like a blow. Already unhappy, the loss of his mother of heroes hit him badly. The effect on Finn was no less great. He had killed scores of times but it seemed as though death was new to him. His sensitive nose on the still-warm body recognised that Tara was never going to move again. What baffled and terrified Finn was the absence of a killing. He gave one more look at his mother's sightless face, now nestled in the Master's arms. Then he turned his head to the heavens and poured out his grief in a long-drawn-out, Wolfhound howl; the most melancholy sound in nature.

The Master had already looked weary and care-worn before he'd called Tara. It was a very grey and sad face he showed as he gently bade Finn go into the coach house and be silent. He had known Tara's heart was weak but had never imagined that his friend would die this way. In a sense, her love for the Master had killed this beautiful hound. Her great love had burst her heart and so the noble daughter of an ancient line had died.

9

A sea change

To Finn, life was never the same after Tara's death. In fact, many changes were afoot, due to the Master's circumstances. They began to take effect immediately after that strange homecoming.

The Master continued to be away a great deal and the Mistress always seemed to be busy and never in a playful mood. Days passed without one of his runs in the countryside behind the bicycle; without a word spoken to him except at meal times. Finn was always locked up at night or he'd have chosen that time for hunting. As it was, the days were his own and he spent less and less time in the house. He'd slip through the orchard, over the gate and stay away for hours, roaming the Downs. For one so large, he became extremely cunning in the pursuit of smaller animals, stalking them cautiously, as a cat would. Day by day, his patience, the most important characteristic of a hunter, grew. Strength was his by birth, but his tireless patience and cunning turned him into a terror to all the wild creatures of the district.

There was just one animal who had no fear of Finn – a large male fox who lived within half a mile. He looked on Finn as a provider of good things. For a long time, this fox grew fat and lazy living off Finn's half-eaten kills. Then one autumn afternoon, Finn saw Reynard leave the shelter of a little wood and pick up a rabbit he'd left in the valley, beside the brook where he'd killed it. Like a flash, Finn wheeled round and gave chase. The fox didn't even drop his meal. Superior knowledge of every leaf and twig in the countryside rather than his own speed won the race.

This interested Finn more than anything for a long time. While his tracking abilities had vastly improved, they were nothing like as keen as those of a foxhound or pointer – Wolfhounds relied on sight and sheer speed for their hunting. But the big fox had grown lazy and had done practically no hunting at all, preferring instead to dine on Finn's left-overs. In fact, this fox had done precious little hunting in his life and regarded himself as the monarch in those parts.

For days, Finn's great interest was in the pursuit of that fox. He began to kill rabbits only if they came his way, but even this was enough to keep the fox in luxury. Finn's first plan was to search for the fox and then give chase. But he quickly realised that the fox was master of this work. His smaller size enabled him to twist and double through places impossible for the hound to follow. So Finn fell back on his recently-acquired cunning. He killed a rabbit and left most of it in an exposed, open spot. Crawling under a clump of brush, he waited with eager, watchful eyes. Before too long Reynard approached from some undergrowth a hundred metres from the kill. But his sharp, sensitive nose wrinkled and pointed skywards. On picking up Finn's scent, he turned and trotted back to cover.

Finn thought long and hard on what had happened. Two days later he tried again, with a much cleverer plan. He killed a rabbit and left it on one of the fox's regular runs. Then he trotted off on the sheltered side of the hill as though making for home. Instead, though, he circled again, carefully keeping to the shelter and flew like the wind to the far end of the run. When Reynard found the rabbit, he merely glanced at it before taking up Finn's trail. At a point as near to the orchard as he dared go, the fox felt satisfied Finn had gone home and retraced his steps.

Reynard picked up the dead rabbit and flung it over his shoulder. He trotted down the path towards his lair where he meant to dine in comfort. At the end of the runway was a wide, open stretch with his cave on the far side. Finn was well-hidden in the bushes down-wind of the fox. His nerves tingled as he crouched, ready for the attack. He waited until Reynard was clear of the runway and well across the open stretch before springing from his hiding place. His leap took him within a metre of the fox. The insolence of easy living and the long record of outsmarting his opponent led to a second's indecision by Reynard on whether or not to drop his dinner. It cost him dearly: on his fourth stride he decided to ditch the rabbit, but by the end of his fifth, the Wolfhound was by his side, his neck bent sideways and jaws stretched wide. As his mouth closed on the fox's back, Finn made his first mistake. Although he was an expert at killing smaller animals, he had no experience of something the size of a fox. His teeth sank deep into the fox's dense coat but broke no bones.

Nevertheless, the force of the impact brought Reynard down. Rolling on the ground he slashed at Finn with sharp white fangs, snarling ferociously. In the same instant, the fox was on his feet, but he failed to get away before Finn's jaws descended on the back of his neck. Gripping him like a vice, Finn shook the fox almost as a terrier shakes a rat. With a desperate squirm the fox wriggled to free himself from this terrible grip. Finn drew breath, holding the fox down with a paw as he did. It was enough to allow Reynard to break free, slashing the loose skin of Finn's chest as he did.

Before he had time to run, Finn was on him once more with a roar of fury. The fox dodged and slashed, opening another wound on Finn's leg. Fighting for his life he wheeled like lightning and flew for cover. But the Wolfhound's blood was boiling now. He swept after the fox as a greyhound chases the hare. When his jaws next closed it was to kill. Reynard squirmed, but Finn threw him over and took a new hold on the fox's throat. Reynard drew up his hind legs and scored Finn's belly. But this wound was the last he inflicted for, as he did, Finn's fangs found the fox's jugular and his warm blood streamed upon the ground.

That was Finn's first big kill. It awoke the Wolfhound's instinct for fierceness that had been hidden for several generations. If the fox had kept clear of Finn for two more days he'd have kept his life. As it was, the slight wounds he inflicted were never even noticed at home. Finn licked them clean and his coat was thick enough to hide them. Besides, the Master and Mistress were preoccupied with other matters.

Early in the morning, a couple of days after Finn's successful hunting of the fox, strange men came to the house, wearing green aprons. It seemed to Finn they were intent on turning the house upside down.

The next day was even more bewildering. In addition to the men in green aprons and noisy boots, many other people strode through the house and gardens as though they belonged to them. Later, these folk gathered in one of the front rooms while one of them stood on a chair and periodically banged a table with a small white mallet. Finn prowled round unhappily, and once the Mistress led him to an empty bedroom where she knelt down on the floor and wept over Finn who tried to lick her, whimpering sympathetically.

Then, silently, the Master and Mistress walked Finn to the station. Their unhappy faces caused Finn to carry his tail so low that it dragged, the black tip picking up mud from the road. That night, and for two more, the three of them lived in a poky room in London. On the third day, they went to another station. This time Finn wasn't allowed in the carriage but had to travel in the guard's van with a mountain of luggage. When a bright, steel chain was attached to his best green collar, Finn felt they must be going to a Dog Show once more.

At the end of their journey, fifty metres from the train, Finn and the Master entered what Finn imagined was the show building. It puzzled him, though, why there were only two other dogs there – a collie and an Irish terrier

– and why they were chained to half barrels filled with straw. His bed looked more as he'd expected it: a flat bench, about thirty centimetres high and well-covered in straw. But it had solid walls and a roof. Before he left, the Master fixed some wirework in front of the bench, shutting Finn in. A notice was hung warning others 'Do Not Touch!'

With a hurried wave, the Master disappeared. 'Wait there, old boy,' he called over his shoulder, rather point-lessly, seeing that Finn was imprisoned.

This had to be the most curious show he'd ever attended. He heard no barking and none of the people passing by seemed interested in looking at the dogs.

After a while, Finn tired of the whole thing. Curling up on his bench, he went to sleep. He woke and slept several times more before the Master and Mistress came to see him. He was allowed out to stretch his legs for a few minutes, but they didn't walk very far. Then he was chained and left by himself once more.

Days passed and all manner of odd things happened. They were obviously not at a show, but whether Finn realised they were on an ocean liner heading across to the other side of the world is unclear. After weeks of hunting free as a bird, the restricted life on the liner developed other aspects of Finn's character – that something which set him apart from other dogs.

For the first few days Finn spent most of his time on his bench, only being taken down for an occasional stroll. Later, when things had settled down into a routine, the Master got permission for Finn to have a good deal more freedom, on the understanding that he was personally responsible for the hound's behaviour. During his hours of liberty, he was never out of the sight of one of his two friends, mostly the Master, as the Mistress was not a good sailor.

Being together so much, Finn grew to understand far more of the Master's speech. He grew to depend on his company and with that, his love of the Master also grew.

With other people, he was more wary. He was polite but reserved, never encouraging their attention.

Before that voyage, Finn had liked and trusted the Master and Mistress. He was thankful for finding them again after his escape, but it's doubtful whether he truly loved them. Now, he would lie for hours listening for their footsteps. When he and the Master sat on deck under the tropical stars, their understanding of each other stopped only just short of actual speech. Their relationship went far beyond the normal companionship between man and dog.

Occasionally, the Master would growl out low remarks about the life they'd left behind in the Old Country, about Tara or their house on the Downs, and Finn would understand practically every word. Then the Master would end by stroking his head and murmuring: 'Ah, well, Finn. There's other good places in the world. That Australian bush is a mighty big hunting ground, I can tell you. We'll have some good times there. Who knows, we might strike it rich and somehow get back to the Downs.'

At such times, though Finn couldn't reply, his understanding was plain to see in his glistening eyes and the eager thrust of his muzzle. Then the Master might say something about the Mistress and Finn would beat the deck with his long tail, as thick as a man's arm. If the weather was fine, the Mistress might come on deck. Finn's eyes would look anxiously if her hand touched the Master's, although Finn was glad to be stretched out between the two of them.

If it hadn't been for the remarkable way Finn's character developed during the confinement of that voyage, it's unlikely he'd have been able to play a part on that dramatic Sunday morning. The weather was very hot and the captain held the service under canvas on the upper deck. Half a dozen children were playing by themselves some twenty metres away. On the back row of the congregation sat the Master with Finn curled at his feet.

Among the children was a curly headed eight-year-old called Tim. This rascal was everybody's favourite and leader of the mischief-makers. How he managed it, no one knows, but a piercing cry suddenly broke through the captain's sermon, and Tim was in mid-air, halfway between the ship's rail and the sea. His little friends were staring horror-stricken where, seconds before, Tim had stood with his chubby arms around the ship's steelwork.

The Master acted on impulse. Finn had leaped to his feet at the sound of the scream. In an instant, he and the Master reached the ship's side. Finn's muzzle thrust between the white rails, watching the little body disappearing quickly.

'Over and fetch him Finn! Over, boy!' the Master urged. Finn knew exactly what was being asked of him but he was no water dog. The sea was many metres below him. He whimpered quietly but the Master urged him on once more.

'Over, Finn, fetch Tim!' he called, swinging his arm excitedly.

The growing love for his Master overcame his instinct. With a snort of protest against the order Finn leaped over the rail. Down, down, down he fell, ten metres into the smooth, blue water rushing past the steel sides of the ship. Once the impulse to act was over, the Master realised that Finn was no lover of the water, that he had never been trained to fetch from rivers. In fact, the Master had never seen Finn swim.

The next moment, the Master acted on a second impulse. Dragging off his coat and shoes and ignoring the shouts behind him, he too leaped over the rail, striking out for Finn and the boy in the warm tropical sea.

Despite his lack of practice, Finn still reached Tim before the Master. He seized the youngster between his powerful jaws, turning back towards the ship. Although he was careful not to hurt the boy with his teeth, he was no trained life-saver and never thought which way up the lad ought to be. When he saw the Master, Finn let go of Tim, preferring to save one he held more dearly. Instantly though, he realised that he shouldn't leave a job undone and returned to the boy. He plucked the child from the water once more. This time the boy's face was fortunately uppermost, but his little arms were trailing helplessly.

It was only a matter of seconds before the Master reached them. The Master seized the boy and Finn seized the Master's arm.

'Down, boy! Get down, Finn,' he shouted. Finn obeyed and circled them anxiously in the water while the Master did his best to keep Tim's head clear of the sea. It was less than three minutes before the second officer pulled alongside in a lifeboat, and hoisted Tim to the safety of the ship's doctor.

'Help the dog in!' shouted the Master as two sailors reached for him. It was a heavy job lifting Finn from the sea but eventually, pushing and pulling, it was completed. Tim was gasping his way back to life across the doctor's knees. It had been a close call.

For the rest of that sunny day there were great celebrations on that Australian liner and Finn came in for considerable flattery. As usual he paid little attention. His heart was still swelling from the little talk he'd had with the Master before the lifeboat had reached the ship. The Master had one dripping arm around his friend's shoulder while he whispered private words in his ear which sent his heart pumping. The Master knew just what Finn had done in the name of love and would never forget it. Finn would have jumped fifty times over to earn those hugs and warm words. The half-hysterical caresses of Tim's mother and the admiration of the whole ship's company were nothing in comparison.

10

The parting of the ways

If Finn had been transported to Australia overnight on a
magic carpet, his first few months in that country would
have been desperately unhappy. As it was, he arrived after
six weeks of steady character-building, and his whole being
was devoted to the love of the Master. And that made all
the difference to the Wolfhound's first experience of the
new land.

Still, it was an unhappy time. The ability he'd gained to
read the Master's moods and state of mind was a burden
that a dog ought not to carry. It was a bad time for the
Master and thus, by extension, for Finn. Some of the evil
events he understood completely; others he could simply
see their effects on his friends.

The first bad news hit them before they'd even left
the ship. They heard that the man in Australia, who the
Master had been relying on for help, had died. So, instead of a warm friendly greeting, they had to fend for
themselves, spending days without a friendly word from
anyone.

The man who had died had been a bachelor farmer, or
squatter as they're sometimes known in Australia. His large
estate and comfortable home was now in the hands of the
Crown who would sell it and pass on the proceeds to
relatives round the world – some of whom had never even
visited the man.

Finn and his family were forced to find economical
lodgings in the city. Over the following weeks, every sort
of misfortune seemed to pursue them, forcing them finally

to move into even smaller and cheaper accommodation, where Finn was admitted begrudgingly.

The Master's walks took him mainly into buildings and offices where Finn could not follow. Had it not been for the Mistress's good care, his life would have been extremely dull. Still, Finn's affection for the Master would have overcome these difficulties and the hours they were apart. But what really sapped Finn's spirits was the growing anxiety and distress filling the Master; the way his friend slumped down at the end of a day, and the lifeless touch of his hand told Finn of the problems the Master was battling.

The climax of these unhappy months came with a serious illness for the Mistress of the Kennels. For weeks it prevented the Master from looking for work. At the end of a most miserable month the Mistress, looking white and desperately shaky, left her bed for the tiny sitting-room. According to her, she would be on her feet in days, but two weeks later there was practically no improvement in her condition. The doctor spoke of a change of air and shrugged his shoulders when the Master hinted at the difficulty of providing such a change.

'I can only tell you she must leave here if she's to get well. A month in the mountains with some decent food would put her right. It doesn't have to cost a fortune.'

Outside the sitting-room, the Master told the doctor, with a certain gruffness in his voice, that his resources were very low. The doctor shrugged his shoulders again.

'Why, you've got a dog there that must eat as much as a man. I imagine you'd have no trouble getting a good price for him. In fact I know someone who'd probably like to buy him.'

'I dare say,' said the Master sadly, 'considering I refused 100 guineas before he was full-grown. That's the finest Wolfhound living. A full champion and the most valuable dog of his breed in the world. But he's not for sale. We couldn't part with Finn.'

'Well that's your business, but I'm telling you that the patient won't get better in this place. I imagine my friend might pay more for the dog; he loves animals and is wealthy enough.'

The rest of the day was the most miserable they'd spent in Australia, but until the Mistress was put to bed, a pretence of cheerfulness was necessary. Then, for many hours, the Master sat before an empty fireplace with Finn's head resting on his knee. Mechanically, he stroked the hound's ears as he thought, but he found only sadness. As the Master rose, Finn tried to show his agreement and understanding.

'It's hard, but I don't see what else a man can do . . .'

Early next morning, before the Mistress appeared, the Master took Finn through the dingy streets where they lived and across the sunlit town to the house of the doctor.

'Doctor, I'd like the address of your rich friend.'

'I thought you might,' said the doctor. 'I'll give you a note for Mr Sandbrook.'

It took them nearly an hour to reach the beautiful house overlooking the sparkling waters of the harbour. They were kept waiting for some time until the portly Mr Sandbrook came to them as they sat on the veranda. Finn was laid out, full stretch, on the cedar floorboards. His head was high and his big dark eyes looked lovingly at the Master. Mr Sandbrook was a good-natured and kindly soul, but he was also vain and fond of giving himself everything he wanted. When his quick, grey eyes fell on Finn he recognised the most magnificent dog he'd ever seen; the most handsome dog in Australia.

The merchant shook hands with the Master and read the doctor's note. He looked at Finn's pedigree and newspaper clippings the Master showed him, as well as a list of championship honours. Mr Sandbrook had made up his mind to have Finn, but he was still a businessman.

'You must realise,' he explained, 'that in this country no dog has the same market value as it has in England. That would be absurd.'

'No price you could offer would normally tempt me into parting with Finn. It's only circumstances that are forcing my hand. But in any country you like, Finn's value to a dog buyer would be 100 guineas – and cheap at that. He could fetch double in England. But I'll sell to you, sir, for fifty guineas, because I'm assured he'll have a good home here. But on one condition: if I can offer eighty guineas for his return within the next couple of years, you must do so.'

The merchant measured the Master through his little, grey eyes. As far as he knew, no one else in the country had such a magnificent hound. He pictured Finn lying on a rug in the fine hall of his fine house, equal to any stately home in England. But to have someone take his hound away – no, his dignity wouldn't allow it.

'No,' he said, 'I'm sorry but I couldn't think of that. I'll make it seventy-five guineas for an outright sale and that's my last offer.'

The Master thought of the Mistress, white and shaky in the dismal little room, waiting for the change which was to give her health. He knew there was no alternative. Five minutes later the merchant made out a cheque and the Master wrote a long list of instructions for Finn's well-being. At least Finn had been assured a luxurious home.

'You don't think he'll run away?' asked Mr Sandbrook.

'No, I'll tell him not to,' the Master replied, 'but for the first couple of weeks don't leave him altogether free.'

They parted in the big hall, surrounded by dim portraits looking down. Finn had been eyeing the Master anxiously for some time. Occasionally he'd wag his tail nervously or make a pretence at gaiety. He sat on his haunches on a large rug. The Master bent down on one knee, an arm round his shoulders. Finn gave an anxious little whine.

'Goodbye old Finn. Goodbye my son. Now, mark me Finn. You stay here – stay here Finn!'

Every cell of his body urged Finn to follow his master but there was no mistaking his instructions. The Master had said stay. Finn crouched down, his weight taken on outstretched limbs. As though the whole thing was too much to bear, he buried his nose and eyes between his forelegs, as if the light was dazzling him. It was the kind of obedience a great soldier would understand. Finn remained, hiding his face, but as the door closed behind the Master, a muffled cry broke from him. Part bark, part cry and part groan, the sound struck the Master's ears with a biting pain as he crossed the gravel. It was more accusation than pain and the Master felt shame as well as grief.

Before noon of that day, the Master was on his way to the mountains with the Mistress of the Kennels.

11

An adventure by night

For thirty-six hours after the Master left, Finn mourned silently in the big house. If Finn had been a year younger, the Sandbrook family would have learned first hand about the Wolfhound howl. As it was, Finn's grief was too deep for howls – he knew instinctively that they would not bring back his friend. And while he didn't understand how he had become the property of an Australian broker, he clearly understood that something serious had forced the Master's hand and that it was now his duty to remain in the house overlooking the harbour.

What he didn't accept was a duty to communicate with a pack of people who had nothing to do with the Master. He felt a degree of obedience to Mr Sandbrook, but no wish to become friends with the rest of the household. As a result, the daughters, the lady of the house and the servants all thought Finn a handsome but sulky animal. They showered him with caresses and soft words but Finn ignored them and kept a watchful eye on the door through which the Master had left. When the youngest daughter sat beside him and bent her head close to his, he wrinkled his nose and very gently, he rose and walked across the room to lie with his nose on the mat where the Master had last stood.

He was taken into the garden two or three times on a leash but gave no thought to escape. The first night he couldn't sleep, simply dozing for a few minutes at a time. The next day passed the same way, except that he was introduced to a group of women, none of whom smelled as though they were connected with the Master.

That night Mr Sandbrook announced that Finn seemed to have settled well and would take him for a walk outside without a leash.

On their second tour of the garden they came to the green gate where they'd first entered the property. Suddenly, Finn was full of an overpowering urge to see the Master. His one thought was to run to the lodgings and see his friend. His hind legs bent and in an instant he cleared the five foot gate. Before Mr Sandbrook had the gate open Finn was forty metres down the moonlit road. He paused and looked back at Mr Sandbrook, who was whistling furiously, before pressing on.

He was a little confused by the streets of the city and often had to double back when he lost his way. But before too long he arrived at their old lodgings. On hind legs, he pawed furiously at the front door. When the landlady opened up she was astonished by the hound pushing past and up the stairs to their rooms.

'Sam,' she called out, 'talk about a menagerie, come and take a look at this!'

The landlady's visiting son appeared with a lamp. Together they climbed the stairs to find Finn whining softly.

'Struth, what a dog,' the lad exclaimed as his mother opened the door. Finn plunged forward into the darkness. In an instant he returned and next pawed at the bedroom. This too he inspected before satisfying himself that they hadn't been there for some time. What a blow. He sniffed in despair at the landlady's skirt and even nuzzled her in the hope that she could produce his friends.

'Is he savage?' Sam asked.

'Wouldn't hurt a sheep,' replied his mother. 'Would you like to know where I got him?'

'No. He's not yours.'

'Well I reckon he could be. His master lodged here for two months but left yesterday for the mountains with his sick missis. Come to think of it, he must have sold the dog so he could pay me and the doctor. Now the blooming thing's gone and run off and is looking for him.'

'Well the dog's no use to your mother.'

'Don't know about that. I might hang on to him and keep an eye out for a reward. He must be worth a bit.'

'Too big and blooming clumsy if you ask me,' said Sam, knowing full well Finn had the grace of a panther. 'Tell you what, I'll have to be off in a minute. I'll give you ten bob for him and get him out of your way.'

But the landlady knew her son too well. When he led Finn away on the end of a rusty chain he was poorer by twenty five shillings. In two days Finn had changed hands for seventy guineas and twenty five shillings – neither meaning a jot to him.

He thought vaguely about returning to Mr Sandbrook later on but, in the meantime, this young man seemed to want to go in the other directions. Little did he know he was taking the same route the Master had travelled. He felt completely alone. For no other reason that he'd come from the same house, Finn also felt kindly towards this long-legged young man.

12

The Southern Cross Circus

That first night with Sam was the most peculiar Finn had ever experienced – even more so than when he was kidnapped – and certainly the most restless.

In the first place, it was spent on a moving train and secondly, Finn's bed was in a sort of wooden cage, sheathed in iron, alongside other similar cages. Next to Finn were two bears. They slept most of the time, making little noise except an occasional snort but gave off the most disturbing smell. On his left was an ancient Bengal tiger. He had sores on his elbows and other troubles which made him extremely irritable. The tiger also had a strong smell, even more uncomfortable to Finn than the bears. Sometimes, when the train jolted, the tiger would roll over, crashing heavily into the partition between their two cages. Finn would spring to his feet, every hair erect and lips drawn back from his fangs, ready for any attack.

The smells and sounds penetrated deep into Finn's heart and soul, stirring up long-forgotten instincts. Just how far back they reached it's hard to say, but they may well have reached the time when Finn's forefathers had been sent to fight against lions and bears, as well as human gladiators, in the arenas of Rome. A wiser man than Sam would have regretted putting Finn in that cage, especially when he was so new to him.

In the small hours, Finn's part of the train stopped close to a little mountain station. At daylight, as Sam went to release Finn, the wagons were already being off-loaded on to carts, ready for the next stage of their journey. This was the famous Southern Cross travelling circus and Sam was an employee of Mr Rutherford, the owner. Sam's plan was to sell Finn for a handsome profit of say £15 or £20. But when Sam saw Finn's fierce appearance he lost his nerve and decided to leave Finn where he was for the time being, until things settled down.

Being shifted from the train and along the bumpy road worked old Killer, as the tiger was called, into a frenzy of rage. As the tiger's actions became more violent, so did Finn's. When the tiger snarled and thrashed his tail, Finn snarled and barked. His legs stiffened, as did the long hairs down his spine. His fangs were totally exposed and saliva began to collect at the corner of his mouth. His unreasoning anger made him look twice the size and it's little wonder that Sam left him where he was.

In fact Sam marvelled at his own courage in leading this monster through the streets. His mother had given him his name and breed, but looking at the hound now all he remembered was 'Irish Wolf,' the title he went under when shown to Mr Rutherford.

'He's the Giant Irish Wolf, boss,' said Sam. 'The only one left in the world, I'm told. I bought him cheap and got him into the cage single-handed. And now I'll sell him cheap to you, boss. If you don't want him, he goes to Smart's; the manager there has offered me twenty-five quid.'

The great John L. Rutherford got quite a thrill as he looked at Finn. He'd lost one of his lions recently through illness and felt that the menagerie lacked something really fierce and bloodthirsty. Like Sam, he'd never heard of a Wolfhound or seen a dog of this size and strength. To anyone who didn't know him or realise the circumstances that had brought on this fierceness, there's no doubt that Finn was an awe-inspiring and magnificent sight. His cage was two metres high, yet Finn's feet came within centimetres of the roof as he plunged and snarled at the partition between him and the tiger. Crouching in the corner, as though about to spring, his black eyes blazed fire and fury, his gaping jaws snarled and his whole body twitched with killing passion.

'Well, Sam, he sure is a dandy wolf,' said the astonished Mr Rutherford.

Sam began to feel what a fine fellow he was. 'As I said, I got him into the cage single-handed, boss. I reckon it'll take the Professor all he knows to handle this brute.'

The Professor was the world renowned Professor Claude Damarel, tamer of lions, also known as Clem Smith.

'Well Sam, it was smart of you to get the beast and you shall have your fifteen pounds. And if the Professor makes a star of him you'll get a rise, my boy. Touch him with that stick and see how he takes it.'

Sam poked a pole through the bars and prodded Finn in the side. Whatever it was seemed to come from the tiger's cage; Finn whirled in a flash, teeth sinking deep into the tough wood until it cracked.

'If he ain't the two ends and the middle of a jim-dandy rustler from way back,' cried Mr Rutherford. 'Go and find the Professor, Sam. Tell him I want to see him straight away.'

The great, barred cage, with its three compartments, was now within a high canvas wall in the centre of the camp. All around were other cages and props from the circus. The circus opened that night and much had to be done to build up the circus ring inside the big tent. A group of piebald horses stood quietly, nosing idly at the dusty ground. Unlike Finn, they were totally familiar with the sounds and smells of the wild animals and no longer paid them any heed.

Sam arrived with the Professor. He wore knee high boots, a bright red shirt and a well-worn leather coat that almost reached his boots. From his right wrist dangled a long whip of rhino hide. In some ways he could be said to be cruel, not in the sense that he enjoyed inflicting pain, but certainly as a means of getting his way. As he approached, Mr Rutherford stirred up the tiger and hence fired up Finn once more.

'What do you think of the latest? How does the Giant Irish Wolf strike you?'

The Professor examined Finn with interest.

'I can't see you training this one much,' said the boss craftily.

'I'd like to know what's going to stop me,' replied the Professor. Have you forgotten who it was who tamed the Tasmanian Wolf, Satan; and a Tasmanian Wolf is about as fierce as you can get after the Tasmanian Devil. Tame this giant Irishman? You bet your sweet life I will.'

'Right-ho, Professor, but I better be on hand just in case you need help.'

'Help! Me need help! You wait here two minutes and I'll show you.'

The boss smiled at the way he'd wound up the Professor. For five minutes he strolled around until the Professor returned with a brazier full of burning coals and an iron rod with a tough leather handle at one end; the other end was buried deep in the fire. Grasping the handle, the Professor opened the cage and slipped inside. Finn was crouching in the far corner. If the light had been better, the animal tamer might have seen that Finn's intelligent expression was not that of a wild beast. On the other hand, his face was still covered in froth and his coat stood on end.

For a moment or two the Professor glared steadily at Finn. He certainly had nerve, believing as he did that Finn truly was a ferocious wolf. Slowly, Finn rose, preparing to meet his visitor as a friend, even as a possible rescuer. The Professor's plan was mapped out and not to be varied. If he had been a waverer, he'd have lost his life many years before. In the instant that Finn started forward, the Professor smacked Finn across the head with the red-hot iron. 'Down Wolf!' he cried, as a pungent smell of burning filled the air.

One part of the iron had caught Finn's sensitive muzzle with the most excruciating pain he'd ever experienced. At the same moment, a terrific snarling came from the tiger. Half-blinded and wholly maddened, Finn sprang at the

Professor with a snarling roar. The red-hot bar met him in mid-air, biting deep into the soft skin of his lips and stinging the silky tip of an ear. The pain was terrible. The smell of his own burning flesh was even worse. The deadly attack from a man was beyond Finn's understanding. Finn sank to his haunches and howled. The boss looked on at the Professor in admiration.

Had Finn really been a wild animal, he'd have probably remained cowering as far away as possible from that terrible bar of fire. He might still have done this had the Professor not raised the bar threateningly once more. Finn had greater reasoning power and a stronger will than a wild beast. He was robbed of all restraint by the Professor's cruel actions, which were totally opposite to what Finn expected between man and dog. The sound of the tiger, his own burning flesh and the Professor's pitilessness filled him with fury and awoke his warring instincts. Despite this, he was able to reason. As the iron bar was lifted for the third time, Finn leaped in under it like lightning. With a roar of defiance he brought his tormentor down, the bar clattering from the man's hand out between the bars of the cage.

Finn planted both feet on the Professor's chest. At any moment the man expected Finn's jaws to close around his throat. He folded his arms below his chin in protection. Next door the tiger was furiously clawing at the partition, roaring and snarling in the most blood-curdling way.

'Draw him off with a stick!' the Professor shouted. Even then he was more concerned with his pride than any injury. Sam jabbed viciously at Finn's face. As the hound moved back slightly, the Professor wriggled free and escaped through the gate. Finn growled threateningly but didn't move. He was only thankful his ordeal was over.

The Professor was bruised but had no scratch or bite. Dusting off his leather coat, he simply didn't realise that Finn had chosen not to hurt him, although killing the man would have been easy. Instead it gave the Professor the opportunity to boast.

'Did you see? He didn't dare bite me. Have no worries, I'll tame that beauty all right. Giant Wolf or not, I've handled worse than him.'

And all this just a couple of days after the young Miss Sandbrook had been rejected while trying to rest her curly hair against Finn's head.

13

The making of a wild beast

The change that began in Finn during the night he spent caged up next to the bears and the tiger was accentuated by his encounter with the Professor. If some wicked scientist had deliberately set out to turn a Wolfhound into a wild beast, he could hardly have taken more effective steps than those which had been adopted with Finn. The mere fact of being caged for the first time in his life, worse still, between two sets of obnoxious-smelling creatures, affected Finn the same way as a nervous man would have been affected if flung into a cell surrounded by raving lunatics.

Shortly after the episode with the red-hot iron, the Professor returned with Sam who was carrying a large, blood-stained basket. From this the Professor took a hunk of raw meat and pushed it through the bars of Finn's cage. A bone was also passed in and a pan of water. The Professor watched closely and was surprised that Finn didn't fling himself on the food. Next door, Killer was raging at the sight of meat, his roars keeping Finn's hackles on end and his fangs bared.

Killer's meat had barely touched the floor before he swept it up and began to tear at it, keeping up a steady growl in the process. But he dropped the meat as if it burned when the Professor demonstrated his powers to Sam by brandishing the iron bar at the tiger. On the other hand, when Finn saw the bar he jumped forward in defiance, bristling at the Professor.

'We'll keep those two together all the time,' said the Professor. 'Old Killer works him into a fine lather. The punters will love him. He's the finest looking beast I've seen in the wolf line. What I don't like about the beggar though is that you can't reckon what he's thinking. He doesn't fly at you straight away, he doesn't even go for his grub. He seems to be turning things over. He's going to be a hard case to tame, Sam. But he's come to a hard-case tamer, don't you forget it.'

If nothing else, the last twenty-four hours had robbed Finn of his grief at losing the Master. It was now thirty hours since Finn had eaten and three days since he'd had a proper meal. In the past he was used to meals from spotless dishes and food a man could eat. But hunger finally triumphed; with a furtive glance, Finn carried the meat to the back of the cage, tore it into strips and ate, much as a wolf would have done, with the blood trickling between his jaws. To drink, Finn was forced to stand close to Killer's cage. He approached the bars snarling, fangs bared. Killer, though, was full. He'd crushed his bone to splinters and eaten them. Now all he wanted was to sleep.

The day dragged slowly; the lack of space and hygiene distressed Finn. As the hot afternoon drew to a close, men came and hitched the cage to a team of horses. Killer woke with a start and began to thrash the partition with his tail. Finn leaped to his feet and answered in similar fashion, the two of them snarling and snapping at each other, making the men roar with laughter.

The wagon moved with a jerk. Soon it was lined up alongside several others in a canvas-covered alleyway, through which the public reached the main tent. This double row of cages was there to impress the audience, a kind of foretaste of the glories they were about to see.

Just then, Finn became aware of a grinding sound at the back of his cage. A sharp, bright point of steel entered the cage above his head. The steel wormed its way through Finn's cage before reaching the partition on Killer's cage. The drill was so quiet that Killer was unaware of what was happening. The hole was Sam's idea, one he hoped would put him in credit with the boss. He took a thin, iron rod, wrapped with bloodied sacking at one end. His plan was to get Finn's scent on the sacking and then use this to provoke the tiger. With John L. Rutherford looking on, Sam wiggled the rod into Killer's cage, rattling it around to attract the tiger's attention. As soon as he saw the intruding object he flung himself at it. Snarling, he challenged the Wolf to come forward or be branded a coward. The rod was pulled away and Finn's massive weight crashed against the partition, answering with a roar of defiance. The great Wolfhound stood on hind legs, snapping at the air with foaming jaws. The boss applauded loudly and gave Sam a shilling for beer.

Two hours later, as the audience filed by and Sam had whipped up the two animals into a perfect rage, a faint odour crossed Finn's nostrils and a faint sound fell on his ears, cutting through the din and commotion. Suddenly, as though he had been shot, Finn dropped from his erect position. He bounded to the front of the cage, an appealing whine replacing the more familiar growls. He'd heard a few spoken words from a woman in the crowd.

'I can't bear to watch. Let's hurry straight in.'

In a passion of anxiety and grief, Finn poured out a succession of long-drawn-out whines. The woman he'd heard was the Mistress of the Kennels, holding tight to the Master's arm as she hurried past the cages. Something seemed to crack in poor Finn's heart as the only two people he loved disappeared from view. Here, in Finn's living hell, the light of his life had passed within a few metres of him. For a long time, Finn gazed out miserably between the bars. He sniffed hopelessly and slowly retired to the far corner of his cage, his muzzle between his paws.

14

Martyrdom

It may be that much of man's wisdom comes from times of grief and suffering. Certainly Finn learned much following that evening when he came so close to being reunited with his friends. His mind could only think that the Master had chosen to ignore his plight and walk straight past him.

When all was dark and silent, Finn fell into much-needed sleep. He desperately needed rest to aid his healing and recharge the energy that had been drained from him. In the morning, Killer's snarls woke him but, this time, he chose to ignore the tiger except for a brief baring of the fangs and a harsh snort. This mild response cost Finn far less vitality than the previous day, leaving him better prepared for the ordeals that lay ahead.

If Finn had been a wild beast, life would have been so much easier for him. Quickly, he'd have learned that the Professor was an all-powerful tyrant and would have accepted that he was to be obeyed. Instead, his instinct told him that the man should be his friend. In the same way, if the Professor had known this, his relations with Finn would have been much better. As it was, all Finn saw was a man completely beyond the pale; a monster disguised as a man; a devil who met friendship with savage blows from a magic weapon. As he saw it, the Professor was out to destroy him.

It goes without saying that the next few weeks were hell for Finn. He suffered horribly at the hands of the Professor who had sworn to turn this wild animal into a docile circus performer. The boss jeered at the Professor's failure to tame Finn within a week, adding greatly to Finn's ordeal. The trainer's pride had been challenged. He made no more public claims but swore to himself that he would break the Giant Wolf's spirit or kill him in the process.

He never guessed that his failure rested on one initial mistake. Instead of the red-hot bar being a sign of power, to Finn it was an instrument of treachery.

On one occasion it did occur to the Professor that the iron bar was somehow standing between him and his mastery of Finn. Leaving the iron outside the cage with Sam, he entered armed instead with his whip. By now Finn totally mistrusted the man, having been tormented by him for two whole weeks. Yet without the bar in his hand, Finn made no hostile move. The Professor walked towards Finn very slowly, words of encouragement on his lips. Just as it seemed he was about to touch the hound, Finn felt he must slip away to the other side of the cage. No snarl or show of fangs but it meant he needed to cross the Professor's path. As he did, the rhino whip came crashing down. Wire had been added to the end, making it even more lethal. The whip cut Finn almost as painfully as the hot iron. He snarled ferociously. Down came the lash again, this time, a piece of loose wire stabbing the corner of his eye. The next instant the Professor was flung back against the bars, his face covered in Finn's hot breath and the sound of his slashing fangs in his ears.

Sam thrust the red-hot iron into Finn's neck, allowing the Professor to grab the bar and beat off the hound. Quickly he slipped from the cage and proceeded to beat Finn with a long hefty pole, his sheer, savage anger powering each blow until his arms ached. Finding no other way to punish Finn, the Professor took away his meal and gave it to the tiger.

By now the Wolfhound was actually very fierce. Scarred from nose to tail with burns and bruises, Finn remained curled in the darkest corner except for the daily encounters he had with the Professor. As the boss said, unless someone was provoking him, Finn might as well have been a lap dog.

Now and then, in the middle of the night, Finn would stand by the front of his cage, drinking in the cool air, his eyes soft with tears. At the end of an hour or so, he'd walk – four paces this way, four the other – occasionally testing each bar with his teeth but always, with a sigh, returning to the corner.

Despite the sadness that filled him, Finn would always meet the Professor with courage and ferocity. Short of starving him or killing him outright with the iron bar, the trainer could see no way of breaking that fierce spirit. Without trying, had anyone known it, Finn would have been a great asset to the circus. But now, all that the Professor wanted was to conquer and master the animal, making him jump through hoops or walk on hind legs.

One day, the Professor was too busy to deal with Finn. Sam fed him in the normal way – the one bright spot of his captivity was the continual diet of raw meat, keeping his condition good. Finn waited for the Professor's arrival, steeling himself for the daily struggle. That night he slept better than he had for many days. The next morning the boss walked by with the Professor.

'I reckon I've given that brute the best. If you want him killed I'll do it gladly but your Giant Wolf's no good for the show,' the trainer admitted.

'He sure is a sulky brute. That writer chap from the city said he wasn't even a wolf, said he was some kind of dog.'

'You should ask the gent to get in the cage with him,' replied the Professor defensively. 'He wouldn't be writing too many more books!'

If the Professor had continued his daily attempts to dominate Finn, there's every chance he would have succeeded. Finn was losing strength and getting close to breaking point. The Professor decided on one more onslaught, more out of revenge at having been beaten. The iron bit deep. His limbs were aching and sore as he stepped from the cage. The Giant Wolf might have bettered him but he'd remember the price he had had to pay.

Finn lay in his corner, quivering and shuddering. He didn't even have the heart to lick his wounds until long after the circus had settled down for the night.

They were camped on the outskirts of a fairly large town – the twenty-second Finn had visited. The authorities had refused permission for the boss to come any closer, so on one side was the dense bush stretching almost as far as the eye could see, back to the mountains. Closer to the town the trees had been ring-barked and were now ghostly skeletons, naked of any leaves, dead bark peeling from the branches.

The moon rose above the trees, highlighting their sorrowful appearance. Finn rose painfully and staggered like an old man to the front of his cage. For almost an hour this tortured prince of animals stared out into the night, big clear drops forming in his eyes, running down his muzzle and pattering on the floor. Although near the limit of his endurance, his brave spirit lived on, forcing him into his nightly habit of testing the bars. The latest attack had injured his nose and forelegs badly, making it difficult for him to make his inspection. Try as he may, the bars still refused to give. Finn sat on his haunches, dreaming for a quarter of an hour before rising to return to his corner.

Something caused him to look out over the treetops to the world beyond. Sore though he was, Finn stood on his hind legs, feet against the gate and only narrowly escaped tumbling through the gate to the ground below. In his anger, the Professor had slammed the gate shut but had forgotten to slip the two bolts. The gate fitted tight, so Finn had missed his tormentor's mistake on his earlier inspection. But his weight had done the trick: there it stood before him, wide open.

For a moment Finn's heart filled so sharply that he was unable to move. But in the next instant he dropped quietly to the earth and was lost in the inky shadow of the main tent.

15

Freedom

Finn moved through the circus encampment like a wolf. The field was aglow with bright silvery moonlight, but not a glint of silver touched Finn's outline. His body was sore and aching from his wounds and stiff from his long confinement. He knew that everyone ought to be asleep but he was taking no chances on being recaptured.

He stood in front of a wide patch of bright moonlight. Pausing, Finn looked round with great cunning, until he found the least dangerous route for him to take. Then, reminiscent of the old Finn, he skipped from one shadow to the next with the lightness of a cat, even though every landing jarred his stiffened joints.

Round the enclosure was a three metre high canvas wall. An attempt to jump and scramble over such a high obstacle would have been noisy and might have led to his discovery. Instead, he thrust his muzzle under the canvas and worked it from side to side until he wriggled out into the open. Only the boss's lazy fox terrier made any sound that night, and his feeble cries couldn't be taken as a warning.

Finn streaked across the thirty metres of moonlit meadow and disappeared into the dying trees, clearing a metre high barbed-wired fence without a pause.

Although Finn's first concern was to put as much distance as possible between him and the circus, he was amazed by the variety of wildlife living in the bush. The leafless trees had allowed low lying vegetation to grow well, making the perfect habitat for many small creatures. All around there were rustlings, and whisperings, tiny

88

footfalls and scufflings amongst dead leaves. Here and there the Wolfhound glimpsed rabbits and bandicoots, kangaroo-rats and small marsupials – all paralysed with amazement at the flight of this strange creature rushing through their territory.

The ring-barked country was soon left behind and Finn found himself slowing considerably as he climbed steeply through dense bush. Besides the thick undergrowth and heavy trees, there were occasional boulders and innumerable fallen trees. Dawn was just breaking when Finn emerged into a stony glade at the top of the Tinnaburra range. His sides were heaving and his tongue hung out. The last hundred metres had been a noisy scramble and Finn found he'd disturbed a family of brumbies or wild horses. The rather flea-bitten old stallion who led the pack protested at this intrusion. Despite Finn's whining note of explanation which meant 'No need to fear me, I'm busy with my own affairs and they don't include you,' the stallion was taking no chances. His chisel teeth were bared and his long tail billowed out behind him. His black hooves rose and fell like hammers on the dewy earth.

Finn had brought a baffling range of smells with him, including men and unknown wild creatures which the stallion neither recognised nor wanted to meet. So the horse continued his mincing march towards the hound, whinnying that this was no resting place for dingoes. The fact that Finn was twice the size of any dingo, and larger than any dog the horse had ever seen, was immaterial.

Finn was in no mood for disputes of any sort. Instead, he made a wide detour, keeping the nervous old stallion happy, and made a descent of the ridge on the southern side. As the sun cleared the horizon, Finn stepped from a clump of wattle and dropped down wearily on a broad, lichen-covered ledge, glinting in the sun's first rays. From here, Finn looked down the dense mountain-side, out over a well-timbered plain to the next range of hills, some eighty kilometres away.

Finn had already slaked his thirst in a chattering stream some distance back. Now he was weary beyond belief. He had been sick and sore and hopelessly out of condition when he'd started out and had now been travelling for six hours. This place gave him a sense of security. The very fragrance of the air told him it was far away from men. At the edge of the ledge was a shallow sandy hollow, screened from the sun by a feathery shrub. He eyed this invitingly before stepping cautiously into the shade and coiling into a ball.

Finn half opened his eyes many times during the day. Once, he was utterly amazed to find a huge wedge-tailed eagle sweeping by, no more than three metres away, with a lamb in its claws. The day was almost over when Finn clambered to his feet and stretched his aching body. Some of his pains were still sharp but the open countryside gave him a deep feeling of contentment. Drawing deep breaths of grateful pleasure, he set off up the Tinnaburra in search of supper.

Before Finn had travelled a kilometre he made his first acquaintance with the snake people. Skirting a fallen tree, Finn accidentally scraped the tail of a carpet snake, almost three metres long. Before he knew what had happened, the snake was coiling its body round Finn's hind leg. As Finn wheeled in his tracks the snake's head rose and spat out a defiant 'Ps-s-s-s-t'. The tightening clamp on his leg caused Finn to panic but, luckily, it encouraged him to take precisely the right course of action: he feinted towards his captured leg and then, as the snake plunged in the same direction, Finn's jaws flashed back and caught the snake just behind the head. One bite was sufficient, for it smashed the snake's spine, almost severing it. In a moment his teeth released the coil around his leg and he was free. But Finn was too shocked to make a meal of his attacker, which is what he ought to have done. Instead, he took a last long look at the brightly-coloured body and then was glad to be on his way. Now though, Finn travelled with much more caution. He had been very lucky not to have made his first encounter with one of the many deadly poisonous members of the snake family.

Finn's experience had rather unnerved him. He thought back to the other strange animals he'd seen since his escape. Just then, a laughing jackass began his hoarse chuckle above Finn's head and a white cockatoo, startled by the jackass, flew screeching from the branches of a big grey gum tree.

But despite being careful, he seemed clumsy in this strange land and the local wildlife had no trouble avoiding him. By chance, he met a creature unlike any he'd seen before – a large, female rock wallaby. Her little one was playing and feeding some distance away when the sound of Finn's approach was heard. It took the baby a second or two to reach the safety of his mother's pouch; just enough time to give Finn a brief glimpse of this strange creature disappearing in two-metre bounds through the scrub. Finn almost sat on his haunches in astonishment.

As strange as it might seem, a feeling of loneliness came over Finn. After the army of menfolk and animals at the circus, the bush began to haunt him, and Finn felt increasingly isolated. It was now thirty hours since he'd tasted food and almost as many since he'd seen any wildlife that could become a meal. Finn carried many instincts to fight savagely under persecution, but few practical instincts in the matter of making his own way in the world. As it was, the aggressive snake, the screaming birds and the half-flying wallaby combined with the huge wilderness to give Finn a depressing sense of outcast. Also, he was getting very hungry.

While these thoughts were troubling Finn's mind, the country he was travelling through became more open, more like neglected parkland. Many of the trees were dead, the rustling streamers of dead bark giving them a curious tortured look. On top of his loneliness, a sudden pang of horror hit him at the sight of a barbed-wire fence, just like the one he'd leaped after leaving the circus. Could it be that the circus had moved on during the day and brought the barbed-wire with it? Finn prowled up and down the fence for a few hundred metres, sniffing and peering suspiciously into the distance. Finally, he leaped the wire and continued in a south-easterly direction.

Five minutes later he saw a rabbit and though he lost it because it was sitting within feet of its burrow, the familiar sight cheered him immensely. A moment later, he stopped dead in his tracks and took cover under thick scrub. He'd topped a little rise and come into full view of a bark shanty. In front was a bright fire beside which sat a man and his big black dog. A steaming billy-can hung from a tripod over the flames. If the wind had been in the opposite direction, he'd have surely been detected.

The man was a boundary rider and his dog a mongrel kangaroo-hound. What impressed Finn most was the picture of the dog stretched out peacefully at his master's feet. Every now and then, the man would cut a chunk from his damper or a slice of meat and toss it to the dog who'd open his jaws like a steel trap, gulping down the morsel without any sign of emotion. The sight and sound of munching reminded Finn's stomach that he was hungry. Almost unconsciously, he crept nearer and nearer to the shelter, his hind quarters gathered tightly, ready to spring.

There was absolutely no reminder of circuses in the scene Finn saw before him. But his recent experiences had been too painful for him to regain his old trustfulness. Even hunger wouldn't make this Wolfhound trustful. Nevertheless, there was something in the scene round the camp-fire which drew Finn. Strangely, this was the first camp-fire he'd ever seen. The flickering flames brought back memories of the Master and the earlier happier days.

By a strange coincidence, as Finn thought of the Master for the first time in many days, five hundred kilometres away the Master strode up to the big house overlooking the harbour. Just as the doctor predicted, the Mistress of the Kennels had regained her health and strength in less than a month. The third week in the mountains had also given her a new friend. She'd met the wife of a local squatter who was spending a few weeks in the mountains with her family. Before the week was out, the Mistress had been invited to make her home with the squatters so that she could supervise the children's education and help the wife with her interest in breeding dogs.

The squatter offered the Master work, but not the kind that would make anyone's fortune, and it was turned down. Shortly afterwards he was invited to join a prospecting party, looking for gold, copper and silver. Within weeks, the prospectors had pegged out many rich claims. First, they took all the surface gold they could find in the streams – the Master's share amounted to £260. Then the party went to the city with the intention of selling the claims to a mining company.

Prospecting fever had gripped the Master and he decided to stay with the party on its next venture. In the meantime, while in the city, he was taking the opportunity of visiting Mr Sandbrook with the hope of regaining his Wolfhound. The merchant was away but one of the daughters explained how the sulky dog had run away and never been heard of since. She showed the Master a reward poster and made it clear that her father had paid dearly for the doubtful privilege of having a dog for two days – a dog who thought his new owners were no better than the dirt under his feet.

The Master made his apologies before walking back to the city with a heavy heart at the loss of the great Wolfhound he so dearly loved. Nagging at his mind was the feeling that perhaps money wasn't everything after all. He handed over most of his earnings to the Mistress and went back to his fellow prospectors.

16

The domestic lure

As Finn drew close to the camp-fire, the smell of stewed mutton sailed down the breeze into his nostrils. But his desire for food was nothing like as strong as his desire to avoid capture. All the while, his limbs were gathered beneath him ready for flight.

Suddenly, a log on the fire broke in half and a long tongue of fire leapt skywards, illuminating a wider circle of bush. At the very same time, the man's dog turned his greyhound-like head and spotted Finn. In an instant, the man's gaze followed the dog's and he too saw Finn. The dog leaped to his feet and barked loudly. Finn jumped backwards in surprise.

'By ghost!' said the man as the kangaroo-hound bounded forward. It wasn't in Finn's nature to run from any dog and so he held his ground. Still full of hostility, Finn prepared to spring, his lips drawn back. But Finn apparently didn't impress the dog. She knew for sure Finn wasn't a dingo and besides, she was a brave creature herself. Certainly the kangaroo-hound was much smaller than Finn, but at seventy centimetres, she was still bigger than most dogs. Showing not the slightest fear, she flew straight at the Wolfhound, barking loudly and snapping at the intruder. As Finn jumped to one side, he became conscious that he was up against a female aggressor. His jaws promptly closed and as the dog snapped a second time, he meekly turned his shoulder to her and gave a friendly whinny.

94

Still the bitch snapped but now more out of ceremony than real business. Finn was obeying the law of his kind when confronted by a dog of the opposite sex.

After a minute, the kangaroo-hound stopped snapping and began sniffing curiously at Finn. At this the Wolf-hound drew himself up proudly, remaining perfectly still and erect. His long tail curved grandly and his head was held high, except for when he had the opportunity of sniffing in turn at the bitch.

During these elaborate formalities, the boundary rider had been watching quietly from beside the fire. He'd never seen anything like Finn before, but felt sure it was a domestic dog and not a wild animal. He pictured himself hunting kangaroos with Finn and Jess (his own dog) – an idea which appealed greatly. Picking up a piece of mutton he took a couple of steps in Finn's direction.

'Come on, boy,' he encouraged in a friendly voice. 'Here then, come on in fellow.'

Finn eyed the man hesitatingly for a moment. The meat was tempting but Finn's memories were strong. As the man advanced, Finn stepped backwards while Jess skipped around playfully. The man was the first to tire. He stopped and tossed the meat to Finn. 'Here then, boy. Eat it there if you like.'

But to Jess, this was taking things too far. Quick as a flash, she dived in and swept the meat from under Finn's nose.

The man walked back to his shack, calling both dogs as he went. Jess ran to him obediently before dancing back in encouragement to Finn. The man took his seat by the fire. Nothing that Jess could do would get Finn any closer to the flames. Realising this, the man ordered Jess to lie down beside him. Cutting off another hunk of meat, he threw it towards Finn, carefully dropping it some metres short. Finn sniffed the enticing fragrance. After all, the man was sitting and it would take him some time to get to his feet. Slowly and warily, his eyes fixed on the man, he covered the ground, seized the meat and sprang back.

The warm mutton was marvellous. The next piece had him closer and then still closer until he stood no more than about two metres away from another piece of meat held in the man's hand. Finn waited but the man wouldn't throw it. With his black eyes fixed intently on the boundary rider, Finn lowered himself to the ground. The man took this as a step forward and rewarded him with the meat. Finn half rose to gulp it down but lay back once more.

The man smiled. 'Well, sonny,' he chuckled, 'you're not taking any chances are you? How do you fancy one of Wallaby Bill's tombstones?' The man flung Finn a solid chunk of heavy damper bread which disappeared in two or three grateful bites. This was the first taste of anything other than raw meat for some months and he enjoyed it. 'I suppose your belly has got a bottom to it somewhere,' the man laughed. 'Here, take the lot.'

With that he pushed what was left of the meat and damper in a tin tray as far as he could towards Finn. Bill then began to busy himself filling a pipe of tobacco while watching Finn from the corner of his eye. The dish was now some three metres from Bill and a metre and a half from Finn. The man appeared to be occupied and Finn's hunger still needed to be satisfied. Very cautiously he advanced on the dish until he could grasp it in his teeth. Pulling it back half a metre, Finn began to eat, watching the man all the time from under his eyebrows. Finn polished the plate clean and then disappeared into the shadows.

'There's gratitude for you,' growled Bill. But knowing animals as he did, Bill remained seated. Finn had gone only as far as the water hole he'd seen, some thirty or forty metres away.

With a little less caution than before, Finn approached the camp, licking his dripping jaws. 'All right, Jess,' said Bill, 'you go to him, then.' Jess came prancing towards Finn who crouched low, ready for action. Jess now imitated Finn's stance and when their noses were almost touching, she bounded away teasingly. Barking in pretended ferocity, she wheeled round before striking the same pose once more.

Wallaby Bill watched in amusement as the two dogs played their game. Had he seen Finn just two days earlier, with foaming jaws, raised hackles and straining limbs, the change would have impressed him even more. Sharing in the pretence, Finn growled deep in his throat while Jess snarled and barked, but when he put his great paw on her back it was with the same gentleness that he'd have handled a pup.

Bill's pipe had long burned out when they tired and lay down on the ground. When Bill rose and stretched his arms, Finn now moved only slightly. In the firelight, Bill could make out the larger of Finn's scars where the Professor's iron had burned through the wiry coat.

'Well wolf, you're the biggest thing in your line I ever did see,' said Bill, 'and you've had a pretty rough time with somebody.' He took a step forward and Finn jumped back three. 'Keep your hair on, sonny, I only want to wash the dish after Your Highness.'

Bill's notion of washing up was distinctly primitive. Taking a last swig of tea, he swilled what was left around the plate. Finn was reluctant to sit down while Bill moved around.

'You just take it easy,' said the boundary rider. 'I'm turning in now and I don't attack thundering great wolves while I've got me trousers down. Just you remember, my boy, where I sleeps I also breakfasts and if you're lucky there might be a few odd bits for great big, grey wolf-dogs as well as kangaroo bitches. So long, old son.'

With that the man disappeared into his shack, and lay down on a bed of sacks stretched over saplings. As for Finn, the man's food and quiet conversation, not to mention the black dog, had given him a strong feeling, something like affection, although a long way from complete trust. Finn didn't lie down again until his ears told him the man was settled for the night.

Well fed and cheered by the company, Finn rested a happier hound than he had been since he'd lost the Master. It was a pleasure to drift off to sleep with Jess's regular breathing in his ears and the warm glow of the smouldering log fire on his half-closed eyes.

17

The Sunday hunt

Finn's new friends were an odd pair. Wallaby Bill had once been a small farmer or 'cockie,' but whenever he received a cheque for his crops or stock, he'd go into town and blow the lot on beer. Afterwards, he would have to buy flour on credit and eat kangaroos or rabbits while his stock scrounged whatever they could manage. It was inevitable, then, that Bill's farming life would be short-lived.

His present life could only be described as nomadic. He was an excellent boundary rider; shrewd, capable and far-seeing. For weeks, or occasionally for months, he and Jess would do their work checking the fencing of the large farms, some as big as an English county. Then he'd head for town and wouldn't be seen outside the hotel until all his cash was safely inside the pub's till.

Bill had reared Jess by hand with the aid of a cracked teapot and the kangaroo bitch knew Bill better than anyone. For her, Bill was the only human who counted; it was said she came close to killing a publican who tried to rifle Bill's pockets while he was drunk.

Bill was not a mean or cruel man, although sometimes he could be rough. Normally, he displayed a careless, good-humoured face. To Finn he seemed a good sort of bloke, of a type that was strange to the Wolfhound. Six months ago, Finn would have accepted Bill's good nature without thinking, but now everyone was treated with suspicion.

The Wolfhound was the first to wake, his movements stirring Jess from sleep. Together they stretched and walked round the camp. Then Finn trotted off towards the dense bush. Jess followed for a little way before turning back to the camp. This surprised Finn but didn't change his plans. He'd noticed a little ridge up ahead which looked as though it might be a home for rabbits. He skirted round the spot so that he approached from the rear with the stealth of a cat. Peering over the ridge he saw three rabbits cleaning themselves no more than about twenty paces from the bank. Finn assessed them carefully before deciding that the middle one carried most meat. Gathering himself, he leapt. As he landed, ten paces from the rabbits, they scattered – two flying diagonally for the banking and the middle one dashing straight ahead. This rabbit planned to run in a wide curve back to the burrow. Finn, though, was expert in the pursuit of rabbits and had learned to wheel sharply, cutting off corners. Two seconds later, the rabbit was dead. Holding it firmly in his jaws, Finn trotted back to the camp at a leisurely pace.

As he arrived, Bill was emerging from the shack, yawning and stretching his muscular arms.

'Hello there, Wolf,' he greeted lazily, 'the early bird's caught the worm, hey? Good on you, my son.'

Finn had stopped dead at the sight of the man and now Jess bounded towards him, full of interest. Finn dropped the rabbit, quite prepared to share his breakfast with her. To his surprise, she grabbed the rabbit and scampered away.

'Come here, Jess!' growled the man sharply. 'Drop it.'

With one or two cuts, Bill expertly skinned the rabbit. Putting the skin on one side he cut the rabbit in two and fed it to the dogs, making sure Finn got the slightly larger portion. As the hounds fed, Bill washed and then made his own breakfast. Jess ate alongside the man but Finn retired some twenty metres away.

After breakfast, Bill went in search of his horse. It was never tethered, but carried a bell so Bill could find it. The two dogs followed – first Jess and then Finn – some distance behind. Jess would keep running back to Finn but she couldn't encourage him to go closer. Once Bill was mounted, Jess seemed satisfied to leave thirty metres or so between her and Bill, allowing the two dogs to run together, sharing their discoveries and interests.

Bill rode a good many kilometres that day, always alongside the wire fencing. If he found a break or a sagging fence pole, he would dismount and fix the damage. While Bill was busy, Finn and Jess would roam wider but never more than a kilometre radius. On these excursions, Finn began to pick up bush-craft from the wily Jess. Once she snapped at his shoulder and pushed him away from a log he was about to clamber on. As Finn stepped back in surprise, a short, black snake reared up and hissed angrily, before darting to safety. He'd seen his first death-adder, a snake whose bite kills in fifteen minutes.

Another time, when a sudden pungent aroma sent Finn scurrying through the undergrowth after the funniest looking creature he'd ever seen, Jess joined in the fun. The iguana had a tail more than twice its body length. And though it escaped with its life, it wasn't quite agile enough not to lose the last foot of tail to Finn's teeth. Having said that, it's fair to admit that only the fastest of creatures could escape the two hounds working together. This reptile managed it by running straight up an iron-bark tree and hiding fifteen metres above the ground.

After four days of learning bush-craft practically every hour of the day from Jess, Finn began to feel as much at home here as he did on the Sussex Downs. But still, his relations with Bill hardly progressed at all. Certainly, Finn could see he was friendly enough, but he had points in common with the circus folk whose behaviour was burned into his very soul. It was a delight to run with Jess during the day and rest by the fire at night, but nothing would induce Finn to go within a metre of the man's hand.

The fifth day of Finn's stay was a Sunday and Bill's day off. He was a strict, if unorthodox, observer of the Sabbath. Straight after breakfast he washed the shirt and vest he'd worn during the week and hung them out to dry. He then brought in his horse, giving it a little treat while examining his feet. After an early lunch Bill set off hunting.

He had no gun, only a formidable sheath-knife, his horse and Jess. In a way, he now had Finn as well. All week he'd wondered about Finn's skill as a hunter and now he had the chance to test out the hound.

The previous day Bill had paid close attention to some tracks he'd seen. At the time, Jess had wanted to investigate immediately. 'You've got your almanac mixed up old girl. This is Saturday.'

Now, with a tomahawk clamped to his saddle, and a stock whip in his hand, Bill set out on his roan-coloured mare to see what the tracks revealed. Jess, full of excitement, circled the horse's head for some minutes. 'Sober up, Jess!' Bill hissed, and the dog fell in beside Finn. At the gully where they'd seen the tracks, Bill slowed to a walk and peered closely at the ground. It was Jess who found what they were looking for – fresh evidence of kangaroo. Finn watched the discovery with keen interest. He noted every little scratch on the trail as Jess nosed them. The long breaths he inhaled also picked up the same scent which hung on the path.

Jess led, Bill followed and Finn, still an apprentice at tracking, brought up the rear. They followed the scent for five or sex kilometres before Jess pulled up suddenly and gave a single bark. Next instant they were all galloping for a thick clump of scrub standing alone in a comparatively open stretch. On the edge of this scrub, Finn caught his first glimpse of their target: an old, male, red kangaroo, quietly grazing on the leaves.

The kangaroo covered over six metres in his first leap. By the time the hunters reached the spot, he was two to three hundred metres away, travelling fast over open country. Bill urged his horse on faster. Finn was close at hand. He could have passed them but still wasn't sure of the man; he felt safer having him in full view.

The red kangaroo seemed confident that he'd out-run his pursuers and made no attempt to dodge them. After the first kilometre his confidence seemed misplaced; the distance between them was now only 100 metres, despite the enormous bounds he made. He could take a fallen log without hesitation, but whenever the ground rose, his speed dropped off.

At the end of the fourth kilometre, Jess, running like a greyhound, was no more than six metres from the kangaroo. Bill was a little further back and Finn was running alongside the horse but somewhat wider. In his eye was a fierce killing light. In that order they entered a steep gully which the kangaroo could have avoided had he been on familiar ground. Plunging down to the bottom, but fearing the climb, the red kangaroo turned along the bottom of the gully. With a bark of triumph, Jess wheeled after him, while the roan mare, forced to turn slower, let Finn shoot through into second place.

Unfortunately for the kangaroo, he'd entered a blind alley and Jess knew it. Before too long, the old kangaroo was faced with a sheer rock climb. With no alternative, he turned to face his pursuers. It might have been the sound of Finn's powerful strides close behind, added to the excitement of the four kilometre chase, that made Jess behave recklessly. Whatever the reason, Jess flew straight for the kangaroo's throat with barely a change of speed. Her reward was a savage kick from the kangaroo's powerful hind legs full in her chest, sending her flying backwards five metres, blood spouting from her.

Finn had a full view of Jess's reception. In a flash he saw the old kangaroo's unusual form of defence – a cow-like kick from legs armed with claws like chisels. He swerved sharply from his course, and leaped for the kangaroo from the slightly higher level of the gully's bank. The old Kangaroo weighed 108 kilograms and measured three metres from tip to tail. But against that, he was sitting still while Finn came at him with all the momentum of his powerful spring. Sixty-three kilograms of bone and muscle, with not an ounce of surplus fat, hit the kangaroo with a tremendous impact. Still he wasn't bowled over, although he rocked alarmingly. Finn had a murderous hold on the red's neck while his great claws were planted firmly in the poor animal's side.

The kangaroo struggled desperately to free his hind leg sufficiently to rake at Finn. Had he succeeded, things would have been grim for Finn. As it was, the Wolfhound was employing the whole of his strength in pulling back the kangaroo's head with the aim of breaking his neck. An old kangaroo such as this would normally have given a good account of himself with four or five Jesses, but he'd never been up against the like of Finn.

We'll never know if Finn had the strength to overpower the kangaroo. With a suddenness that surprised Finn, Wallaby Bill sprang from his horse, leaned across Finn from behind and slit the marsupial's throat with his sheath knife. Finn growled fiercely on feeling the man's weight and sprang clear the instant the kangaroo fell down dead.

Not realising it was the man and not he who had killed their quarry, Finn turned his attention to Jess. The black hound would do no more hunting for some time. Finn was already licking his friend sympathetically when Bill turned away from the dead kangaroo. Hackles rising, Finn slipped out of reach. He had been disturbed by the contact he'd had with the boundary rider's arm across his shoulders.

With a single blow, the kangaroo had ripped open the whole of Jess's side, as deep as the bone in places. The furrow in her belly looked as if it had been caused by an axe. Bill sighed as he examined the damage, wondering if Jess had any real chances. Any surgeon would have been greatly interested in what Bill did next. First he collected water in his hat from a nearby hole. Cleaning the wounds as best he could, he opened a pouch hanging from his belt. Taking out a needle and some strong white thread, in a matter-of-fact way, as though mending a shirt, Bill began to stitch up Jess's wounds. During the whole operation, the black hound barely moved, just a faint motion of her head once or twice, as though she was trying to keep an eye on Bill's progress.

Then, Bill filled a pipe and smoked for a while. Presently, he brought more water in his hat, holding it under Jess's muzzle so she could lap a little with her tongue without having to move too much. The gratitude shining in her eyes was unmistakable. Bill waited a while longer and then scooped Jess up in his arms and carried her carefully all the way back to the camp. Finn followed twenty paces behind, his head and tail hanging low.

At the camp, Bill made a bed of leaves for Jess and then wrapped her up in an old coat in such a way that she couldn't reach her wounds. Then, Bill remounted and rode back to the gully. When he returned, the red kangaroo roped to his saddle, he found Finn affectionately licking Jess's muzzle. She hadn't moved an inch.

18

Three dingoes went a-walking

Bill proved to be a kind and shrewd nurse where his one close friend was concerned. Jess was extremely ill and too weak to interfere with his actions. Even the slight lifting of her head to lap a little broth seemed to tax what strength she had. All night Finn lay within a few metres of the black dog and in the morning he brought a fresh-killed rabbit to her. Finn meant well, but Jess didn't even have the energy to lick the offering. Bill took it away, and skinned and boiled it for Finn.

'You're a mighty good sort,' Bill said, 'and you can say I said so.'

After making Jess as comfortable as he could, Bill rode off to do his day's work. He'd rigged a shelter over her, made from some lengths of stringy bark. He gave her a breakfast of broth and left a dish of water by her nose. Bill looked back over his shoulder once or twice to see if Finn would follow, but the Wolfhound stayed where he was. When the man was almost out of sight, he lay down beside his friend.

Finn's life moved into a very interesting and pleasant phase, divided evenly between keeping his friend company and foraging in a five or six kilometre radius of the shack. Little by little, he learned the secrets of his patch.

Eight kilometres away, due south, lay the big, old, rambling homestead belonging to the station (the Australian name for a ranch). Jacob Hall, the bachelor who built up Warrimoo station, had died six months earlier and the property had been passed on to relatives from overseas.

Jacob had always been a little eccentric. He'd been a great student and admirer of animal behaviour. When the rabbit population began to get out of hand, he'd amused his neighbours by importing twenty-five pairs of ferrets and weasels and turning them loose amongst the rabbit burrows. These fierce little creatures terrorised the region's poultry but totally ignored the rabbits they were meant to control.

Jacob Hall had then imported a pair of wild cats and let them loose. He also encouraged domestic cats to revert to the wild. At great expense, he even succeeded in finding a pair of Tasmanian Wolves and Tasmanian Devils and smuggling them in past the customs and quarantine officials. These bloodthirsty creatures were let loose and never seen again. Soon after, it was said that certain changes were occuring in the local wildlife. There was talk of extra large cats and dingoes with the untameable fierceness of the Tasmanian Wolf about them.

Naturally enough, Finn and Jess knew nothing of these things. Jess's prime concern was the return of her master and Finn was occupied with his exploration of the bush. Neither of them knew that they themselves were of great interest to a very large circle of wild folk.

Within twenty-four hours of the kangaroo hunt, news had got about among the wild folk that a formidable hunter had been laid low and was near to death. As Jess had always been well fed by Bill, she had no need to pursue small game for food. But she had taken many a wallaby and played her part in the death of numerous kangaroos. Now it was the chance of the possums, wombats, koalas and bandicoots to leave their cover for a glimpse of the hunter they feared so greatly.

News spread to the hills, and during the second night three dingoes left their hunting ground to look into the matter themselves. Once they came within a couple of miles, they began to advance with extreme caution. Moving like shadows, they eyed every leaf and twig on their trail in case it held danger. In the dying light of the smouldering camp-fire, the dingoes saw Finn's wiry outline. His place beside the fire meant this monster was no dingo. He had to be a giant amongst wolves, connected in some way with men-folk.

After spreading more terror through the district by making their kills, the dingoes settled down to watch Finn. When dawn broke, they saw Finn rise, stretch and then make off from the camp. The dingoes looked at each other. Perhaps this giant was a wild relative of theirs after all. He certainly had no mind to face the man in daylight. Then with hackles raised, the dingoes saw Bill emerge and walk over to see to Jess.

As it happened, Finn stumbled across a fresh wallaby trail which he followed with growing excitement. The hunt took him a good deal further from the shack than he'd been since his first arrival, which meant that by the time Bill was ready to leave for the day, Finn was nowhere to be seen.

'I guess he's after an extra special breakfast of his own,' muttered Bill, 'but I'll leave him this bit of rabbit just in case.' The patient dingoes watched closely, licking their chops as Bill ate and again as he placed the cooked rabbit on a log. These proceedings were also of interest to several crows. It was as protection against them rather than the weather that Bill had erected the bark shelter. Otherwise, as Bill knew well, it wouldn't have been long before Jess lost her eyes.

After Bill left, the crows were the first to descend, soon having the meat meant for Finn shredded and swallowed. Then, they swaggered impudently round the fire, picking up crumbs. The presence of these wicked black scavengers gave courage to the dingoes who decided it was safe to investigate the dying hound they'd heard so much about.

Still cautious in every step the three dingoes advanced, marching abreast. When they got within twenty-five paces Jess got wind of them and it occurred to her that her final hour had arrived. She knew she couldn't run and doubted if she could stand. In agony, the helpless bitch rolled over and raised her head so she could see her doom approaching. She gave a little gulp upon seeing that there were in fact three full grown dingoes advancing. Stocky, massive in the shoulder, full-coated and with fangs made for killing, their eyes had the killing light in them. A snarl curled her lip as she pictured her end, knowing full well the dingoes would never dare attack had she been fit.

Very slowly, in a fan formation, the dingoes approached. With a valiant effort Jess managed a bark which ended in a howl as the pain stabbed through her. Jess glared out at them, her fangs bared and her short hair on end. The dingoes assessed her probable strength. There was also the shelter to consider. But the biggest of the dingoes had once stolen a sheep from a shepherd. Since then, he felt less fear of man's domain. He advanced in front of his comrades, which spurred them on in turn. As the dingoes drew near, Jess braced herself to die biting.

As the first dingo's snout poked its way under the bark Jess managed to hunch further back against the shack, intending to draw the dingo in a little more and give herself a better chance of grabbing some part of her attacker. With a desperate effort, Jess managed to draw herself up almost into a sitting position. Her faint groans of pain were a real help in a way, as they made the dingo reckless, thinking that the bitch was close to death.

In the instant the big dingo went for her throat, Jess latched her jaws on his foreleg. The snarling, terrified dingo snapped at her neck. Outside, the two remaining dingoes let out yelps of pure terror, wheeled like lightning and streaked into the scrub, bellies flat to the earth. The arrival of Finn was almost magical. He was dragging a young wallaby and had first stood still on catching a glimpse of the dingoes until he realised that they were attaching his crippled friend. He made no sound but flew over the clearing with deadly speed. As he reached the shack a frightening roar burst from his chest, putting the two dingoes to flight. Finn followed close behind until a kind of telepathy stopped him dead and he almost somersaulted as he turned to go back to

Jess's aid. As Finn plunged forwards, the dingo desperately managed to wrench his leg free. But as he turned, the big dingo from the hills found himself facing Finn; he knew he would have to fight for his life.

The dingo has been called many cowardly names but when at bay, it becomes as brave as a lion. Finn, a towering figure of blazing wrath, stood glaring at the dingo. He'd made one kill that day and his blood was running hot. The thought of these wild dogs attacking his helpless friend made his blood boil. Rage almost blinded him. He flung himself forwards only to learn that creatures bred in the wild are swifter than the swiftest of other creatures. He should have known, having witnessed how the kangaroo dispatched Jess. Finn only grazed the dingo's haunch but he received an eight centimetre wound in the same movement. Even while in the act of turning, Finn felt the dingo's fangs ripping through his skin as though it were stretched silk.

Finn's anger wasn't lessened but the blind rage was. He pulled himself together with a jerk, a cold determination to kill cooling his brain. This time, he allowed the dingo to come forward, which he did, aiming for Finn's lower legs. This movement opened up the back of the dingo's neck. Finn plunged for it and missed with the breadth of two hairs. He pivoted and feinted a blow for the dingo's leg who in turn aimed a cutting snap at Finn's thigh. A master fighter, the dingo deliberately tries to cripple rather than to kill too quickly. The move, though, gave Finn the chance he'd worked for. Next moment, his great fangs were buried in the thickly furred coat of the dingo's neck and all his weight was bearing the wild dog to the ground.

His legs gone, a frenzy of despair flooded through the dingo. He fought like ten dogs, snapping and scratching and despite Finn's vice-like hold the dingo inflicted considerable damage with his razor sharp fangs on those parts of Finn's body he could still reach. But the race was lost. Finn gradually shifted his hold until he found the soft part of the throat and then bit with all his might.

Closer and closer his jaws came together till the dingo's blood flowed to the ground and the wild dog's struggles got fainter and fainter. With a final great shake of his head, Finn lifted the dingo clear of the ground and flung him backwards, limp and still.

For two whole minutes Finn stared at the body, licking the blood from his lips and working his torn skin into place. Then he turned to look at Jess. As he did, the dingo opened his glazed eyes, dragged himself to his feet and staggered feebly towards the bush. A startled cry from Jess warned Finn to turn round. Amazed, he saw the creature he thought he'd killed was still alive. Five seconds later though, Finn made no more mistakes. The dingo was on the ground, its throat torn out.

'Well by ghost!' exclaimed Wallaby Bill when he returned to the camp. 'If I didn't tell that Wolf this morning what a good sort he was. My oath, a steam hammer couldn't kill that blessed dingo any more.'

Finn had been too busy tending Jess and licking his own wounds to think about feeding. That night Finn was served like royalty on wallaby steaks and damper. But even on this special occasion, Finn refused to come within touch of the man.

19

A break-up in Arcadia

The dingo's attack put Jess's recovery back, but before the week was out, Bill had removed his crude stitches and the wound showed every sign of healing cleanly. Yet, despite the kangaroo-hound's considerable hardiness it was almost another week before she was able to move round the camp. It was another ten days before she resumed her old activities.

All the while, Finn played the part of loyal protector. The wild folk of the bush became very familiar with Finn as he patrolled their range, learning every twig and trip of country in the process. The snake folk – brown, tiger, carpet, diamond adder – all became known to him, studied from a respectful distance. One evening, for instance, Finn saw a carpet snake pin a big kangaroo-rat against a fallen log. With a speed he could hardly follow, the snake twisted two coils round his prey's shining body, and crushed the life from the little creature. Then, slowly, almost as if enjoying it, the snake worked his coils down the length of the body from head to tail, breaking all its joints and crunching the body flat. Then, also slowly, first using the top jaw and then the bottom, the snake swallowed the kangaroo-rat whole. Just as the snake finished, Finn sprang from his hiding place and killed the snake with one bite. Bill was just dismounting from his day's work when Finn arrived with a three-metre snake in tow.

On another occasion Finn came across a koala strolling across the clearing. Finding that the fat, little creature offered no fight, but instead moaned and cried like a distressed child, Finn made no attempt to kill it. He picked the koala up by its loose skin and dropped it at Jess's feet, and for the rest of the day, he and Jess amused themselves by playing with it. The game was one-sided to be sure; the poor little fellow was rocked to and fro by the hounds' muzzles, sobbing and moaning grotesquely. Bill laughed when he saw their antics but called Jess off and let the koala go free.

About a week later, when Jess had been following her man in the same way as before, both hounds began to notice a change in Bill's behaviour. He never took the slightest notice of Finn and rarely looked at Jess. When she approached in the evening he'd gruffly tell her to lie. He even went so far as to push her away with his boot when she tried to lie beside him. Jess had vague recollections of similar happenings that were distinctly uncomfortable. Jess's uneasiness soon became transferred to Finn, making him all the more shy of Bill.

One evening, the surly boundary rider sat by the fire, counting and recounting a wad of money. The day before, he'd visited the station homestead and drawn his wages.

'Get out o' there, damn you!' Bill growled at poor Jess, creeping towards him with watchful eyes. With the mark of Bill's boot on her side, she retreated. She bore no malice and would have died for the man but she was disturbed and unhappy nevertheless.

In the morning, Bill hardly bothered to make breakfast and the clothes he wore Finn had never seen before. He tied up the door of the shack and mounted his horse. For almost fifteen kilometres the two hounds followed, sadness and dread in their hearts. Finally, they found themselves in the wide street of Nargoola township, standing outside the First Nugget Hotel. Bill hitched his mare, strode across the veranda and disappeared inside. Then it all came flooding back to Jess.

Finn remained with Jess some metres from the horse. But whereas Jess was content to lie down and wait, Finn stood erect and watchful. He was much nearer houses than he cared and the air was heavy with man's scent. Finn was uneasy and let Jess know as best he could. She urged patience and tucked her nose further under her legs.

One or two men passed by, making overtures to Finn and gazing at him in astonishment. 'My oath! I guess old man Hall's pets have been busy up in the hills. I wonder how Bill got a hold of him!' As the interested man tried advancing on Finn, the Wolfhound leaped back like a stag, keeping a good twenty paces between himself and the men-folk.

Out of consideration for Jess, Finn endured the discomfort of waiting throughout the day, ever watchful; there among the man-smells and the shadow of the houses, the Professor could have been lurking. But when evening came, and Jess showed no sign of leaving her post, Finn could stand it no more and told his friend that he'd wait for her at the camp.

Jess's nuzzling touches plainly asked 'What's your hurry?' But Finn's mind was made up. He turned his shoulder coldly, although still hoping for a sign that she would follow. But her ties to Bill were far stronger than any consideration she might have for her own well-being and, of course, she didn't have Finn's violent mistrust of man and his works.

In the end, Finn gave a cold bark of displeasure and trotted off into the twilight. Half an hour later he killed a fat bandicoot and a short while later ate his dinner by the camp-fire ashes. Later, he settled down as much as he ever did these days. Dozing, free of all thoughts of men and cages, the bush air seemed sweeter than ever.

20

The outcast

For nine days and nights, Finn lived alone at the camp with no sign of Jess or Bill. Once, when the heat of the day had passed, Finn trotted down to the township but there was no trace of Jess or her man.

Finn had recently made the acquaintance of the koala he'd treated so roughly and now met the quaint little chap every day. For his part, Koala never made advances but seemed to realise that the great Wolfhound meant him no harm. And though they had limited conversation between them, Finn nevertheless enjoyed watching his antics and listening to his chatter.

Another of the wild folk that Finn met for the first time, and continued to meet on a friendly basis, was a large native porcupine, or echidna. Finn met him while sniffing round what he thought were rabbit burrows. The ant-eating porcupine appeared a few metres away, his shock of frightful quills not at all inviting to someone with a delicate nose such as his. Finn and Echidna eyed each other up and decided neither had any inclination to bother the other.

But unlike the majority of Australia's wild folk, Finn was a dedicated meat eater which rather put him at odds with his neighbours. In particular, Finn would have enjoyed the company of bandicoots but they and their kind always had it in mind that they were a potential meal for the Wolfhound. Therefore, full or empty, hunting or lounging, Finn was seen as a scourge and an enemy to be avoided at all costs.

It was on the evening of the tenth day, while resting in preparation for his hunt that Finn woke to the sound of horses hooves approaching from the south. He could detect none of Jess's scent but this had to be Bill returning. As usual, he took up a position where he could observe Bill in safety. As the newcomer dismounted, he caught a dim glimpse of Finn and mistook him for a dingo, and a monstrous one at that. The man was indignant that a dingo should display such cheek. Uncoiling his five metre stock whip, he swung it round his head and flung it at Finn with all his might, catching Finn in the ribs.

'G-r-r-r, you thieving swine! I'll teach you!'

The voice was strange to Finn, very hoarse and harsh. The Wolfhound cantered off and the rider followed him right into the scrub before returning to the camp.

From the shelter of the bush, Finn watched the man gather twigs and light a fire, just as Bill would have done. He heard grumbling and swearing from this man who had been moved from a post he had liked to this place which he didn't like at all, because Bill had left the district. Had he been less unhappy, the man's reaction to Finn might have been different. As it was, by driving Finn away he had reinforced the wildness of spirit the circus folk had planted in him.

Finn wanted nothing from man's society. All the time he'd been at the camp, Finn had fended for himself. But now he was being told that even the camp was forbidden to him. Man had declared war on him. All that was left was the wild.

The wild gave him unlimited food and interest. It was clean and free, restricting him in no way and offering little or no hostility. Altogether, Finn was confused and bitterness and resentment filled his mind. Vague thoughts of the Master flitted through his head as he watched the man. Even now, his natural forgiveness made him forget his humiliation. Slowly, but with no particular caution, Finn stepped graciously towards the camp, intending to take up his old resting place, twenty paces or so from the fire. No sooner had he entered the light from the flames than the man looked up.

'Well I'll be damned if this ain't the limit!' he gasped, springing to his feet. He snatched up a burning branch from the fire and, rushing forward, flung it so accurately that it fell across the Wolfhound's neck, singeing his coat. A rock followed the fire and the man followed the rock. Flying sparks and the smell of burning were sufficient for Finn without the added humiliation of the rocks and curses. The hound broke into a gallop, shocked beyond words. Snarling as he ran, Finn didn't stop until the camp was some kilometres behind him.

The incident with the burning branch made a deep impression on Finn. For thousands of years man has driven off wolves from their home territory with the use of fire. Finn had never experienced such behaviour, but in some strange way he seemed to know of it. For 1500 years Finn's ancestors had had a place by the side of man. But now, the man's message was clear – he was being sent to his place and his place was the wild.

The wild folk of Tinnaburra will never forget that night and the madness of the one they thought of as the Giant Dingo. For four hours Finn raged furiously up and down an eight kilometre belt of country, slaying and maiming at will, fixing a dreadful fear in the hearts of all those who lived in the area. By chance, up in the rocky hills, Finn met one of the two remaining dingoes that had attacked the wounded Jess. It was an evil chance for that dingo. A fanged whirlwind smote him, tearing him apart before he realised what had hit him. In his fury, Finn even leaped into a tree, pinning a defenceless possum into instant death before leaping down once more.

When the wild killing spree was finally over and Finn lay down to rest, there was not a living thing that didn't live in dread of the Giant Dingo. It was a night that would be remembered alongside bushfires and earthquakes. And all because the Irish Wolfhound had been hounded out of the men-folk's world and into the wild.

21

Mated

If Finn had deliberately thought of the worst way to
start his life among the wild folk, he couldn't have done
better. When he set out the next morning, every one of
his regular hunting trails was deserted. Not so much as
a mouse was to be seen. The only exception were the
crows and laughing jackass who jeered at him from
the stump of a stringy bark tree. The natural scavengers
had already removed every trace of the carnage he'd left
the night before. Finn had no other option but to curl up
and sleep on an empty belly.

Finn didn't know it, but hundreds of small bright eyes,
full of fear and resentment, had watched him as he ranged
his trails. Finn's actions had made him guilty of a real
crime according to the standards of the wild folk. Had he
been a lesser creature, swift punishment would have been
meted out. As it was, he was left to work out his own
punishment by finding that his hunting was ruined. The
wild folk instinctively understood that meat-eaters needed
to kill to survive, but there was no place in their society
for wilful slaughter.

When Finn awoke, it was to the sharp reminder of
his hunger. Before long, he also sensed there was a solid
atmosphere of hatred all around, although it took him
some while to realise it was aimed at him. He found
the sensation intimidating. True, he was undisputed lord
of the range; no one could better him in combat. But
the concentrated and silent hatred of the bush struck a
chill in the Wolfhound's heart.

The empty runways spoke loudly of this hatred. The still trees thrust it at him. The sightless scrub glared ill-feeling his way. Finn's skin began to twitch and he found himself looking over his shoulder. When a long streamer of bark rustled behind him, he turned with a snarl. Humiliation swept through his body.

It was with a sense of genuine humility and something like gratitude that Finn met Koala, who was trying to hurry across open ground between two trees. Faced with Finn, Koala stopped dead in his tracks. His tiny hands wavered in grief. Finn whispered assurances and the little fellow sank to his haunches, tears of relief in his eyes. Finn lay down in front of Koala and began to question him on the chilling attitude ranged towards him. In his own fashion, Koala managed to let Finn know that his actions of the night before had made him an outcast, something Finn already knew deep in his heart. Finn gathered that the native wild folk would never forgive or forget.

There were some rabbits feeding in the open a little further on. Hunger drove him to hunt, but there was no pleasure in it. Since being in Australia he had adopted the locals' attitude towards rabbits and had lost the taste for them. Still, he was hungry now. Quickly, he stalked and killed the fattest of the bunch, carried it into the bush and devoured it steadily.

For a good few hours Finn strolled about the familiar tract of bush which had been his home for many weeks. The signs told him that his future here was bleak. He had outraged the wild folk and was being ostracised as a consequence. At midnight a crow and a flying fox saw Finn settle for the night, and quickly passed the word round. At dawn, armed with this intelligence, the small creatures came out to eat, watching only for their constant enemy – the snakes. In fact, they fed so busily that a pair of wedgetailed eagles was able to descend on them easily, picking up a fat breakfast without even trying. Unreasonably perhaps, this loss earned even more hatred for Finn.

For three more days the Wolfhound continued in his old hunting ground, but had to content himself with an exclusive diet of rabbit meat. Even these were becoming more difficult to stalk, so deep had the fear and hatred penetrated into the minds of the wild folk.

On the fourth evening, sad at heart, Finn turned his back on the familiar trails and hunted west and south, heading towards the stony foot of Mount Desolation. For a kilometre or more his evil reputation proceeded him, and it was some time before he sighted an unwary, fat wallaby hare. That night in his den, Finn feasted better than he had since those easy-going days prior to being expelled from the camp.

These few days had changed the Wolfhound a great deal. He now walked with far less gracious pride and with more watchful stealth. He walked more silently, stalked more carefully and sprang with greater speed and ferocity. He was no longer an apprentice but an actual part of the wild. Thus it was, the next afternoon, that he leaped from sleep to wakefulness at the sound of a tiny twig rolling down his little gully. There, watching him, with a curious, eager sort of inviting look on her face was a fine red-brown female dingo, or warrigal. True, she was a good thirty centimetres smaller at the shoulder than Finn, but she was a good size for a dingo and unusually long in the body. Her ruddy brown tail was bushy and handsome, and she carried it high and flirtatiously curled. When her pale, greenish eyes met Finn's she wagged her tail encouragingly. The dingo stood with her feet planted well apart, much as a show dog does. Her tail switched slightly and her nostrils quivered. This belle of the back ranges had heard of Finn but it was only on this day, when nature had recommended her to find a mate, that she had thought of coming in search of the great Wolfhound.

Finn sniffed hard and gave a friendly bark. As he scrambled up the gully towards the warrigal, his own tail was waving high. The dingo ran off a dozen paces before wheeling round skittishly and lowering her muzzle. No sooner had Finn touched noses than she was off once more, teasingly. To and fro, back and forth, the shiny-coated dingo played the Wolfhound. Twilight had darkened into night before she yielded herself to him totally. As is always the case with wild folk, the courtship was brief but none the less passionate. At the time, Warrigal seemed the most desirable creature in the world.

Presently, Finn and Warrigal took the western trail. The dingo pointed out a big bandicoot for Finn who delighted in showing off his hunting skills, stalking and then slaying the creature with considerable flair. Finn gave the choice parts to his sweetheart. Then the two of them lay and licked and nosed, chatting amicably for an hour.

After they rested Warrigal stood up, stretched out her long body and then headed once more for the distant hills. Finn followed as a matter of course. He had no ties binding him any longer. With Warrigal waving her bushy tail in front of him, Finn spared not a thought for Koala or Echidna.

Although Finn knew his own range as well as he could, he knew nothing of the dingo's ways and what had made Warrigal such an important member of her tribe and the acknowledged belle of her range. Out of gallantry, or perhaps because the trail was new, Finn trotted slightly behind his new friend. But while Finn's body was tense, ready to spring, she trod the trail with the casualness of someone who is used to being treated like royalty. The laws of her race prevented her from being attacked by a male dingo and no female cared to face her in single combat.

As they neared the foothills of Mount Desolation, the country grew wilder and more rugged. The bush was much sparser. Huge boulders covered in lichen littered the stony ground. Amongst a stand of shrivelled, peeling trees, Warrigal growled a warning. She would have barked had she known how but it told Finn that danger was near. Two seconds later, he knew exactly the nature of the danger.

A pair of lusty males, aware that Warrigal was looking for a mate, were hiding under cover of the scrub. In an instant, they flung themselves at Finn, one from either side. Warrigal, her tail dragging across the ground, slipped through the action. Stopping a dozen paces away, she sat on her haunches and watched the fight with great interest. Not knowing what to expect, Finn suffered the penalty. Both shoulders were cut to the bone by the flashing fangs of the dingoes. Their target had been Finn's throat but his extra height had spoiled their deadly aim. Wolf-like, they leaped aside after the first attack, not trying to hang on to their prey.

Before Warrigal's watchful eyes there began the finest fight she had ever seen. She was already satisfied with the good looks of her suitor. Now she had a chance to judge his strength in a world where everything was finally decided by the tooth and the claw.

Warrigal watched with the keenness of a show judge. Not a single movement in all the dazzling swiftness missed her expert appraisal. In the first moments of the fight, the two dingoes were drunk with pride. It seemed certain to them that the interloper would perish. In fact, Black Tip took the opportunity of taking a lightning cut at his compatriot in the confusion, feeling it was wise to get what head start he could; once the Wolfhound had been eliminated, there would be a second fight to win Warrigal.

It took Finn some time to realise the exact nature of the situation. But once he settled to his work, he was a terrible foe. He had learned well in the wild and now fought much more like a wolf than he once would have. At first he snapped savagely to one side only. This left the other flank exposed but it allowed him to edge gradually towards a boulder. Once he felt the friendly touch of the rock, his onslaught became double-edged and terrible as forked lightning.

He was kept too busy to think of death blows yet. His opponents' jaws were never far from his neck or forelegs. Finn, though, was beginning to make his mark, slashing the dingoes cruelly round the shoulders and neck. He even managed to pluck Black Tip's ally clear of the ground, flinging him by the neck over a low bush. A piece of his neck remained in Finn's teeth, spoiling the effectiveness of his next attack on Black Tip. But from that moment on, Black Tip's cause was lost, as were all his illusions about the stranger.

When the wounded dingo returned to the fight, his eyes were like red coals and his heart was full of deadly poison. Instead of attacking the throat, he slunk like a weasel round the far side of the boulder and fastened his fangs on Finn's hind leg. Finn was feinting for a death-hold on Black Tip's throat when the sudden fire in his thigh caught his attention. He leaped straight up, dragging the dingo with him. In mid-air Finn twisted free of the grip, landing in a coil with his massive jaws clamped around the dingo's throat. His fangs met. He gave one terrible shake of his head and when the dingo fell, his throat was laid open to the night air.

Finn was bleeding from a dozen large wounds, but Black Tip knew it was no longer possible for him to overcome the Wolfhound alone. The big dingo now turned his thoughts from killing to survival and putting up a fight that would not disgrace him in Warrigal's eyes. Partly through courage and partly through luck, he achieved his aim. Even wounded as he was, Finn could handle the dingo with ease, but Black Tip had the same sort of smell as did Warrigal. Now that the threat of death had subsided, the dingo's scent reminded Finn of his loved one and lessened the desire to kill his attacker. Instead of finishing him off, Finn took hold of his loose coat and flung him aside with a ferocious snarl. With life before him and another chance to win Warrigal, Black Tip was exceedingly pleased to leave the battleground, bounding off into the scrub with a long fierce snarl of his own which he hoped would impress Warrigal.

When it was clear that the fight was really over, Warrigal minced forward to Finn and began tenderly licking his wounds. Her mate had done her proud, fighting valiantly on her behalf. Brave though she was and a fierce fighter in her own right, Warrigal was still a female and she was still able to soothe and flatter her great, grey lord while she tended his wounds with her tongue.

When every cut had been cleaned and antiseptically treated by the two busy tongues, Warrigal slowly moved off down the trail, throwing a coquettish look of invitation over her shoulder. Finn stepped proudly after her.

Immediately below the crest of a sharply rising spur of the mountain, they came to Warrigal's den, hidden by the spreading roots of a fallen tree. The entrance was almost too small for Finn, but he bent his aching body and squeezed himself into a chamber large enough for half a dozen dingoes. Finn sniffed the walls curiously. Finding them embedded only with Warrigal's scent he lay down and sighed with pleasure. Warrigal looked down on her mate in admiration. His long body practically stretched across the full length of the den. After checking over his wounds once more, Warrigal finally lay curled beside him and went to sleep.

Two hours later, Warrigal rose softly and went to inspect the night. The world was bathed in silky moonlight, bright as day but infinitely more mysteriously beautiful. Sensing through her nostrils what was happening in the wild she sat on her haunches and raised her voice in a not very melodious dingo cry. Next instant, Finn was beside her, with lolling tongue and questioning nostrils. Together the pair played like kittens there on the moon-kissed ledge. Perhaps it was then rather than the earlier afternoon hours that Finn courted Warrigal. The sting of his wounds seemed only to add zest to his love-making, after all, they were nothing more than love tokens. Finn rejoiced in his battle scars. He had fought for Warrigal and was willing to fight again. His reward was Warrigal's tenderness and devoted attention. The night air was sweet and the moonlight seemed to run like quicksilver in Finn's veins. Certainly, he told himself, this new life in the wild, this life of matehood, was a good thing.

22

The pack and its masters

When Finn and Warrigal tired of their play, the moon had set and there was the first grey hint of the coming dawn. In that strange ghostly light, which gave even the most common objects a look of mystery, Finn saw two unfamiliar figures climbing towards Mount Desolation. There was a deep, steep-sided gully between him and the strangers but, even over this distance, Finn could sense the hostility directed towards them.

Warrigal was just about to enter the den when Finn touched her nose and pointed out the ghostly figures. Her lip curled, indicating she knew full well who they were. The one in the front was large and heavy and low to the ground. Every line of his frame spelt savagery. His tail was long, straight and smooth, like a rat's. In his slightly parted jaws Finn could see long yellow tusks. This creature was similar in outline to a hyena but with more strength and fleetness in his make up. As the light improved, Finn noticed that the animal had black stripes, like a zebra, on a light yellowish background. This was old Tasman, the Zebra Wolf, turned free by Jacob Hall six years ago and whose mate had died in the first year.

Behind Tasman, burdened by a fat wallaby, marched Lupus, his four-year-old son and the acknowledged master of Mount Desolation. Lupus had none of his father's stripes and his tail was well covered in hair. He was a half-bred dingo but larger and more terrible in tooth and claw. His feet were as deadly as a bear's. His loins and thighs were those of a fleet runner, while every hair of his head and massive chest were those of a killer. Tasman was feared rather as a tradition. Lupus was feared and obeyed as a ruthless killer.

Unlike his father, Lupus had eyes that could face the day. He didn't particularly like the bright light, but it didn't stop him from venturing out and killing during the day. Together, they still shared the den they first found all those years ago. It was said among the wild folk that Lupus had killed his mother so that the two males might survive during a season of drought and poor hunting. Be that as it may, she had given him a place amongst the dingoes and his father had given him his unquestioned rank as leader. Lupus had never openly preyed upon dingoes, but he hadn't hesitated in swiftly despatching the half dozen dingoes who had disobeyed his word.

Tasman no longer hunted, Lupus did that for him. It was even said that Tasman had been seen foraging for grubs and insects. But despite his age, there was no one in that countryside who would have dared to face the old wolf alone.

Warrigal was not able to pass much of this to Finn as they stared out through the grey mists, but what he did gather deeply impressed him. The shudder of Warrigal's shoulders as she turned towards the cave told Finn volumes. It didn't seem fitting to the great Wolfhound that his handsome mate should shudder at the sight of any living creature. So, before following her into the den, Finn stood on the edge of the flat rock and barked fierce defiance at Tasman and his formidable son.

In sheer amazement, Lupus dropped his burden. Both father and son faced in Finn's direction and glared across the intervening ravine. Through the misty half light they could see Finn standing royally erect, his tail curving grandly and his massive head held high. The sight was awe-inspiring and a more formidable picture than any dingo could have made. Tasman and Lupus glared at the interloper for two whole minutes, growling all the while in concentrated fury.

As the light from the east intensified, old Tasman's eyes blinked furiously and his growl died to an irritated grunt. Picking up his kill, Lupus and his father trailed off up the mountainside to their den, full of anger and bitterness. Barking fiercely, Finn watched the lords of Mount Desolation till they were lost among the crevices and boulders. Then, with a final far-reaching roar, Finn entered the den where Warrigal was waiting. Finn's utter recklessness made her skin twitch but it was certainly something to have a mate who cared so much – even in ignorance. Long after Finn lay sleeping, Warrigal watched him with a look of pride and devotion in her wild yellow eyes.

It was well into the afternoon before Finn and his mate went in search of food. Near the patch of barren trees, Black Tip and two friends of his approached. Warrigal growled warningly, but her alarm was misplaced; it seemed Black Tip had spread the news of Finn's arrival without hostility. In fact, the group sniffed each other with exaggerated respectfulness. Seeing their friendly intentions, Finn wagged his tail at which the dingoes leaped back in sudden alarm. Their reaction amused Finn and his great tail continued to beat while he snorted friendly greetings through his nostrils.

After this, the dingoes took heart and there was another round of sniffing and nosing. Then the five of them trotted off into the scrub, Warrigal noticeably close to Finn's side. If, by accident, one of the other dingoes found themselves at the front of the pack, Finn would drop back a pace or two and a quick look from him was sufficient to send the straying dingo back to his place at Finn's side. There was no talk about it but from the beginning it was clear that Finn was absolute master there and that Warrigal had pride of place amongst the rest of the pack.

Finn might have appeared to lead the hunting party but it was Warrigal who was the real leader that night. The previous day she had located a mother kangaroo. Now she wished for two things: a good supper and the chance for her lord to demonstrate his hunting prowess. Black

Tip had learned his lesson, but it was as well that the others saw Finn's might for themselves. Warrigal knew that dingoes feared mother kangaroos more than the old men of the species. Even with two comrades, Black Tip would not have considered attacking the kangaroo if ever there was easier prey to be had.

In due course, Warrigal got wind of the kangaroo and checked her pace suddenly. Silent as ghosts, Finn and the four dingoes stalked their prey between the shadowy tree-trunks, taking a wide arc so they approached from good cover. To Warrigal's disappointment they found the mother kangaroo feeding with a mob of seven others, under the protection of a big old red. Through the mysteries of animal telepathy, Warrigal explained her plan of how they could separate the mother and leave her to Finn, while they distracted the rest of the kangaroos.

Carefully and silently, the hunters got within ten metres of their quarry. Then, with a terrifying howl, a living rope of dingoes – four of them, nose to tail – flung itself between the mother kangaroo and the rest of the mob. The old red gave one startled look of panic and then they were off like the wind in big seven metre bounds. The mother was prevented from fleeing in the same direction by the yowling streak of snapping dingoes. She sprang off at a tangent but on her seventh or eighth bound, with her heart almost bursting in terror, a roaring grey cloud swept on her from the right and she felt Finn's fangs burn into her neck. She sat up and desperately sawed for her life with her hind claws.

The dingoes knew that her deadly chisels would mean death for anyone who felt them. Instead, they surrounded the kangaroo and gnashed their fangs in the hope of paralysing her with fear. But, as yet, they held back. Finn slipped once as he tried to take a fresh hold and he paid for it with a slash to his groin. But the same wound was the kangaroo's death warrant as it filled Finn with fighting rage. A second later, Finn held a broken neck between his powerful jaws and blood mingled with the kangaroo's reddy-brown fur as her heavy body fell sideways, with Finn upon it.

The three dingoes moved towards the kill, but were stopped in their tracks by a snarl from Warrigal and a swift look from Finn. He and his mate helped themselves to the choice hind quarters while the others fed on the front part. There was more than enough for all and when they left the kangaroo for the scavengers, Finn had another good meal between his jaws, intended as a gift for his mate. Instinct told Warrigal that Finn's forethought in providing food for later was a good quality to have in a mate and it pleased her.

That night while Warrigal tended Finn's wound, Black Tip and the others spread the word of Finn's might as a killer. They vowed that a more terrible fighter than Lupus, or even his seldom seen but much feared father, had come to Mount Desolation. The old dingoes shook their heads, feeling they lived in strange and troubled times. Lupus, on the other hand, was ranging trails on an empty stomach in savage quest of the stranger who dared to defy him.

23

Single combat

Even while he hunted, the irritating image of the creature
who had barked at him remained with Lupus. To make
matters worse, he missed two kills and failed to find other
game.

With anger in his blood, he happened to cross the warm
trail left by Warrigal, Finn and the others. This led him
to the remains of the kangaroo, where he disturbed lesser
creatures feeding at ease. Lupus had no mind to leave bones
with good fresh meat on them and when he resumed the trail
there was nothing much left for the ants and mice.

Lupus followed the trail easily. He licked his chops as he
picked up whiffs of Warrigal's scent and remembered why
he had been so interested in them. It occurred to him that he
should have a mate and the Warrigal was the finest choice
around. The stranger had to be removed once and for all.

Before Lupus touched the first loose stones at the bottom
of the hill below Warrigal's den, the inhabitants of the
scrub were well aware of his presence. Following at a
respectful distance were Black Tip and seven other dingoes
who didn't happen to be out hunting.

Halfway up the hill, in the minds of those that followed,
Lupus's unbeaten insolence led him to make a stupid
mistake. He paused and bellowed out his approach with
a harsh grating howl that could be heard a kilometre away.
Then he continued up the hill, careless in his self-confidence
and driven by the desire to have Warrigal as a mate. Lupus
was determined to rid the range of the one who had flung
defiance at him across the gully.

In an instant, the howl woke Finn. He recognised the voice and knew well enough its meaning. He knew that here was a more considerable enemy than he'd ever faced before. There was also a regret that the challenge should come now while his body was scarred with unhealed wounds and his left thigh was stiff from the punishing slash he'd received. In a moment Finn was outside, his deep bark rending the silence of the night. The eight dingoes following Lupus glanced at one another, knowingly. Never was a leader more hated than Lupus. Black Tip and those that had fed on the kangaroo felt sympathy and pity for Finn but like all the others, they were keen to see the fight – and to act accordingly. The question of what would become of Warrigal was on all of their minds.

Huge and fearsome that he was, Lupus had a lumbering mind and was not over-intelligent. When Lupus first caught sight of the creature he had come to slay, he had a moment of uneasiness. Framed against the skyline, Finn's towering form loomed above him, hackles erect and bathed in moonlight. But Lupus knew nothing of fear. Every animal he had met so far in combat had been slain. And now there was the added motivation of Warrigal's powerful scent.

Finn neither advanced nor retreated a single step as Lupus drew nearer. He simply bayed at intervals and scratched the earth with his paw. Once, Warrigal moved alongside him and joined in his snarling but Finn sent her back to the mouth of the cave. The instant Lupus dragged his frame on to the ledge, he plunged forward with the clumsiness of a buffalo. For his trouble, he received a slashing bite across one shoulder and a chest thrust that sent him reeling off the ledge and on to his back on the trail below. A dingo would have leaped upon him then and there and maybe the fight would have ended swiftly. Black Tip and his companions gasped in astonishment. Had Lupus stayed there a second longer he might have had their teeth in his throat. As it was, Lupus learned from the stranger and it was a far more deadly approach he made the second time.

The fan of watching dingoes closed in a little as Lupus remounted the ledge with a blood-curdling snarl and an awe-inspiring show of gleaming fangs. Next instant, the two were at grips and Finn realised he was in a fight for his life. The sheer weight of the wolf-dingo told him that here was a most serious combat. A sense of doom passed through him when his opponent's powerful jaws closed on his upper leg.

Finn retaliated by tearing one of Lupus's ears in half and the terrible grip on his leg relaxed. The Wolfhound sprang completely over the wolf-dingo, taking a slashing bite as he landed. Then the two rose erect in the air, like bears, meeting jaw to jaw. The clashing of fangs sent thrills through the watching dingoes who recognised they were watching the greatest spectacle of their lives. As the combatants dropped back to the ground, Lupus regained the same punishing hold as earlier on Finn's leg, sending a flash of panic into his heart. Only with the most violent twist of his neck was he able to attack any part of Lupus at all. But panic drove him on and his long neck curved sufficiently to take a hold of the wolf-dingo at the back of the head. One of his lower teeth penetrated Lupus's lower jaw; that was the last time Finn's legs were in danger. No matter what punishment his shoulders received, Finn had learned to protect his legs.

Lupus had centred his attack on Finn's throat and seemed prepared to take any amount of punishment to secure an underhold. The dingoes watched in silence, their line moving not an inch. They realised that if Finn was laid low, there was still more fighting to come. Warrigal, too, stuck to her position, but not in silence. A low continuous growl came from her jaws, lips pulled back over glistening fangs.

In this battle, Finn's height was working against him, exposing his throat to Lupus's attack. On the other hand, it facilitated the killer strike he preferred – to the back of the neck, the way a terrier takes a rat. But Lupus was well protected with a thick mass of bristles and rolls of skin over his spinal column. More than once Finn had failed to inflict killing pressure. For his part, Lupus had managed on three occasions to do damage with his slashing claws. One of Finn's veins had been opened and blood was matting with the dust on his coat.

The flow of blood again made Finn fight harder. He plunged at his enemy's neck and Lupus, sitting up like a kangaroo, fended off the attack with his foreleg. A quick flash of bloody, foam-flecked fangs and the deadly paw was crushed between Finn's jaws. The pain drew a screeching howl from Lupus. With an upward flick of his neck, Finn rolled Lupus squarely on his back. In less time than could be measured, Finn released the crushed foot and seized the throat – the deadly underhold. Here the wolf-dingo's bristles were sparse and the skin comparatively thin. Fighting for existence, Finn put every ounce of energy into his grip. Lupus writhed and twisted, like a cat in torment. Finn's fangs sank a centimetre deeper. The wolf-dingo clawed helplessly in space and Finn penetrated another centimetre. Suddenly, hot blood gushed between his fangs. Lupus's great body hunched almost vertically from the shoulders upwards. A hind leg scored a deep furrow but Finn's fangs had met at the red centre of his enemy's throat. There was a faint grunt, a final muscular spasm and Finn stood back, shaking his dripping muzzle. The fierce lord of Mount Desolation had entered the long sleep; his lordship was over.

Finn sank back on his haunches, gasping with foam streaked tongue dangling from his jaw. The watching dingoes advanced two paces. Warrigal, stepping beside her mate, snarled a warning. But Finn gently pushed her aside and through his torn muzzle gave a little whinny which plainly said 'You are welcome here!' With that, Black Tip moved forward respectfully, his tail between his legs. Long and thoroughly he sniffed the dead body of the terrible Lupus before whinnying in turn to his companions. In twos and threes the rest of the pack followed Black Tip's lead, climbing the flat rock to inspect the dead tyrant. As they turned away from the rock, the gestures they made towards Finn were as near to a salute as a dingo could achieve.

When all the dingoes had made their inspection, Finn did a curious thing. Grabbing hold of Lupus, he heaved the body from the ledge to the trail below. 'Here is your old lord,' he barked. 'Take him away and leave me now!' Black Tip and half a dozen others seized the carcass and dragged it down the trail to who knows what end.

For three days after, nothing was seen of the Wolfhound. The bush-folk would see Warrigal hunt each day but left her in peace. Some of the young bloods talked of hunting out old Tasman but the counsel of elders strongly favoured delay. 'Let us wait and see what the Great One will do when his wounds are healed,' they said.

24

Domestic life in the den

For three days, the Wolfhound and his mate tended Finn's many lacerations, accumulated from three considerable battles. When he was not giving his wounds a thorough licking, Finn slept or ate the offerings Warrigal would bring.

On the fourth night, still quite stiff, Finn made a small killing not far from the den. His early life had given him greater reserves of strength than any of the wild folk and from that point on his wounds gave him no more trouble. They healed cleanly and swiftly until they were no longer apparent to the eye. An ordinary dingo would have been obliged to fight many more battles before being granted leadership of the pack. But this position fell naturally to Finn. After all, he'd slain the tyrant, trounced one of the strongest in the pack and killed another, and most of the pack had seen his prowess the night he slew Lupus.

Finn was also generous. Whenever he killed he would take three portions – one for him, one for Warrigal and one for the den. What was left was given freely to the rest of the pack.

No sort of temptation seemed strong enough to take the Wolfhound close to humans. It soon became understood that Finn was not interested in taking sheep, a prohibition the pack felt also applied to them. So, Finn's mastership was a good thing for the squatters and their flocks but not so for kangaroos. No matter how big or strong, they never seemed too much for Finn to tackle. Also preferring large game, the pack began hunting together in a formation behind the heels of the great Wolfhound. Thoroughly enjoying himself, Finn cared nothing for those who fed from his kills, providing he and his mate had sufficient.

Once, two of the youngest members of the pack, not much more than pups themselves, were attacked by an outsider. Bleeding and yelping, the youngsters carried their woes to the scrub below Finn's den. He, Black Tip and a few others quickly followed the trail of this interloper. Within six kilometres hard gallop, the unfortunate creature was pinned to the ground and shaken into the long sleep. This was an act of leadership Lupus would never have done; and something eternally to Finn's credit.

During this time, subtle changes had come over the Wolfhound. Though well fed and certainly under no pressure, Finn had still acquired the hard, spare look of a wild animal. His alertness, wariness and deadliness had made him one of his mate's own kind. He differed from them in his great bulk, his dignity and his generosity. He never argued or issued threats. When warnings were needed he gave them. And if killing was necessary he did it without any fuss. Occasionally, Finn also barked. But in other respects, Finn was a dingo.

Some six or seven weeks after arriving at the den, Warrigal began to change in certain ways. She seemed to be less interested in her mate and less affectionate. She spent more time lying around the den, showing no eagerness to hunt or play. However, life was too full for Finn to worry overly and it was only on occasions that he thought of it. One night, though, he was surprised when Warrigal snarled at him in a surly manner without any apparent cause. All he'd done was to give her a friendly touch with his nose by way of inviting her to hunt for the evening's supper. Finn walked out of the den with as much dignity as he could. In his place a dingo might have snarled and argued for half an hour. He simply decided, in his hurt, that Warrigal needed a lesson in manners. That night he would eat near the kill and she would go hungry.

Finn killed a half-grown kangaroo that night on which he and a few others fed. In the small hours, the Wolfhound wended his way home, prepared to sleep alone unless Warrigal had changed her tune. At the mouth of the den he stooped low, in order to enter, but he was brought to a halt by a long, angry snarl from within. Warrigal was making it very plain that Finn's place was outside. Such an unprecedented outrage angered Finn, but he withdrew to sleep on the ledge, with as much dignity as he could manage.

Just after daybreak Finn was woken by a small, unfamiliar cry. With head cocked to one side, Finn listened. There it was again. Certainly it was not Warrigal's voice though it came from inside. Also, there were a number of other small sounds that were strange -- weak, quaint gurgling sounds. Finn decided to investigate the puzzle.

As Finn stooped low at the entrance Warrigal snarled, but this time without a note of aggression. Instead there was a hint of appeal in the tone -- 'Be careful! Please take care!' it seemed to say. Advancing with extreme caution Finn found his spouse lying full length on her side with her bushy tail curled round the smallest of four sleek puppies which she was nursing diligently. Moving with the utmost care, Finn sniffed round his mate but in deference to Warrigal's warning growls, refrained from touching the puppies. Finn stared at the domestic group, his jaw hanging open and his eyes plainly saying 'Well! Who'd have thought of this! They're nice enough little creatures in their way, but no cause to snarl at your own lawful mate!'

Seeing that Finn displayed no hostility, Warrigal raised her nose in a friendly fashion for the Wolfhound to lick her. Then she gave a little whine and glanced round the empty walls of the den. Finn replied with a quiet, reassuring bark and ten minutes later had killed an unsuspecting rabbit. On his way back to the den, Finn dropped the rabbit and added a bandicoot to his catch so that Warrigal might have variety in her breakfast. Being parched with thirst, Warrigal accepted both gratefully. After she'd drawn some sustenance from the meat, she nudged Finn from the cave and then raced like an arrow for the creek. In less than two minutes she was back, bright drops of water clinging to her muzzle. Considerately Finn had remained outside. This earned him a look of appreciation from Warrigal as she slipped back inside to her puppies, who were already grizzling for warmth and nourishment.

Finn took to his role of father and provider. He lounged at the mouth of the cave, occasionally popping inside to see how things were before returning to keep guard. Finn was now allowed to touch the little creatures but they didn't like the feel of his tongue and wriggled away in their blind, helpless way. As for Warrigal, she seemed absurdly happy and assumed considerable airs of importance.

That night, the pack had to forage for itself. When Finn made his kill he announced in no uncertain terms that there was none to spare for the followers. In the course of the night, it became known to all the wild folk in that range that the mate of the dingo leader had other mouths to feed. For the time being, Finn would do all the hunting for the den on the rock ledge.

25

Tragedy in the den

When Warrigal's pups were born, Finn had been in the Tinnaburra for nearly five months. During the whole of that time, not a single drop of rain had fallen. Now, with the approach of summer, Finn had quite forgotten that there was such a thing as rain. He slept on the earth and accepted its dryness as the natural course of things.

Annoyingly, just as the puppies were opening their eyes and becoming more mobile, the creek at the foot of Mount Desolation disappeared through its shingly bed and was seen no more. This meant a trek of six kilometres to the nearest drinking place, a serious matter for a nursing mother whose tongue always seemed to loll from her mouth in thirst. Warrigal would make the journey there as quickly as she could and drink till she was fit to burst. On the return journey, concern for her family would make her dash for the den where she arrived panting and gasping and more thirsty then ever. The weather was getting hotter and with her full teats and heavy body, Warrigal was in no fit condition for fast travelling. Finn did his part well and thoroughly and there was no lack of fresh meat, but he could not carry water. Finn's mate had no option but to run hard over the parched ground at least twenty-two kilometres a day, and often up to thirty.

One result of these circumstances was that Warrigal's children began to eat meat earlier than normally would have been the case. It was probably Finn's expertise as a hunter that made him realise before the others that the hunting was becoming increasingly difficult. There was still plenty of small prey to be had, but Finn found himself travelling farther afield to find the larger game he needed to feed six hungry mouths.

Then Warrigal returned to the trail. Finn had not failed his mate in the least but now she felt obliged to share the load. The children were still too young to fend for themselves, although by now they were chasing any insect that invaded their rocky ledge.

One day Finn had a stroke of luck in coming across a wallaby, badly wounded in a dingo trap. Had Finn not found him, the poor wallaby would have died a miserable, lingering death. Finn put him out of his misery, slung the body over his shoulder and set out for the den. Just as Finn scaled the rocky ledge a desperate cry of anguish filled his ears from above. It clearly came from one of his children. With a greater thrill of paternal concern than he'd felt before, Finn dropped his kill and leaped in two bounds to the mouth of the cave. As Finn landed, a figure emerged from the mouth of the den bearing in its yellow tusks the limp body of Warrigal's last born son. The figure in the moonlight was the most terrible, ugly one that the country had produced. Thin beyond belief, ragged, bald in spots, old Tasman the Zebra-wolf had his tusks in warm juicy flesh for the first time in three months. He was prepared to pay with his life for the privilege.

Skin, bone and a savage despairing ferocity was all there was left of Tasman, two months on from the death of Lupus. Living on scraps of carrion or on grubs and insects, Tasman had a desperate hunger that had drawn him to the smell of daily kills and young animal life. Now he was face to face with the master of the range and the outraged father of Warrigal's pups.

The gaunt old wolf dropped his prey. In his day he had killed many a dingo, but this grey monster roaring at him now was different from anything he'd ever known. With massive bony skull held low, Tasman let out his most terrible snarl of challenge and defiance. In years gone by, this sound would have paralysed his victims, making them easy prey to his vicious tusks. But as far as Finn was concerned, the growl was powerless. Finn gathered himself for attack, but a scattering of loose stones distracted him. Suddenly, an outstretched furry mass flew across his vision and landed like a cannon ball on the wolf's neck. Warrigal had also returned from the hunt and now Tasman had to deal with the fury of a bereaved mother. Warrigal was a whirlwind of rage, revealing to Finn for the first time the full fighting force that had given her her unquestioned standing in the pack.

With a twist of his still powerful neck, Tasman flung Warrigal from him but as he did, the mightiest jaws in the Tinnaburra closed around the underside of that scrawny throat. Even as the life blood flowed away, Tasman's body was literally being torn apart by Warrigal's busy fangs. Old Tasman was not just killed, he was dispersed, dissolved and scattered as worthless carrion.

Gasping and bleeding, Warrigal wheeled around with a moaning cry and shot into the den. She had already seen one son dead; two daughters lay dead inside and while she licked his lacerated body, the life ebbed from the last remaining son. Still she licked – for almost an hour, though he lived for no more than a few minutes after she'd found him.

Then Warrigal went outside. She found Finn licking the one deep wound Tasman had scored. Warrigal sat on her haunches as few metres from Finn, pointed her muzzle at the moon and poured out her sorrow to the flawless dark blue sky. The Wolfhound listened for some time without moving, until the sadness ate into his soul. Then he, too, lifted his head and delivered the Irish Wolfhound howl; louder, more mournful and carrying further than any dingo cry.

The Wolfhound and his mate never entered their old home again and if you were to visit that cave on Mount Desolation today, you'd probably find the skeletons of three of Finn's and Warrigal's children there still.

26

The exodus

In the early dawn of a blistering hot day, Finn and Warrigal walked slowly down the hill to where the rest of the dingoes lived. Somehow, the news of what had happened had spread and before the sun had properly risen, every single member of the pack personally investigated Tasman's remains.

The lack of water and the poor hunting was beginning to cause considerable distress. Already, a large number of wild folk had gone in search of a better home. Even Finn's skill as a hunter was of little use in the absence of game. The Wolfhound sometimes travelled forty-five kilometres or more without a single kill. Like the others, Finn was reduced to eating rabbit flesh, mice and grubs. Some of the younger dingoes had resorted to preying on the squatters' flocks, a move that had so far resulted in one dingo being shot and two others being trapped and slain. The pack was now down to just fourteen adults and a handful of whelps, still unable to fend for themselves.

Smaller animals were forced to eat bark, thereby killing the trees. This spoiled the hunting and opened up land that had previously been closed to man. In fact, men with guns had been seen within two kilometres of Mount Desolation, something which concerned Finn greatly.

As Finn sat on his haunches, he noticed a degree of boniness that hadn't been there since his dreadful days of captivity in the circus. A growing sense of restlessness and discontent that had been with the pack for some weeks was accentuated when a party of six men on horseback was seen along the foot of the mountain. If the men's dogs hadn't been so stupid in sticking closely to the trail, it's likely that many of the sleeping dingoes would have been hunted and possibly killed. In Finn's mind, this act finally made the range uninhabitable. For hours after the men had passed, his nostrils twitched. As soon as darkness fell he nudged his mate's neck and took to the open trail. The rest of the pack began to gather behind. It seemed to be understood that this was no ordinary hunting trip. Only one old dingo, who had always sullenly resented Finn, cautioned against the exodus. But the pack ignored him and left him sitting on his haunches in the dust. When they were a kilometre or so away the old dingo began to howl dismally; when Finn made his first kill, ten kilometres to the north west, old Tufter was on hand, yowling eagerly for scraps.

Behind Finn's back, Tufter complained vehemently that they were going in the wrong direction. In a way, he was right. South and east were comparatively better watered. Finn knew this, of course. He also realised that men were in that direction too and the memory of how he had been tortured was ingrained in his soul.

Towards morning the pack topped a ridge, a good forty-five kilometres from Mount Desolation. They spotted a small mob of nine kangaroos browsing in the scrub. Finn was after them like a shot, with Warrigal hot on his heels and the rest of the pack streaming behind. There was a stiff chase of some six kilometres and when Finn finally pinned the trailing kangaroo, only five dingoes were still in sight. Even Tufter got a good meal from that big fellow.

Well fed and rested, the pack felt good about following such a fine hunter as Finn. What none of them realised was that the kangaroos they'd seen were also migrating – but in the opposite direction!

For a week the pack moved north west. Old Tufter grew a little more bitter every day – with some cause as it happened. Game was becoming pitifully scarce. The country did not appeal to the dingoes at all, being dry as a bleached bone and totally shadeless. A long exhausting chase enabled Finn to pull down an emu; nothing but beak and feathers remained when the pack moved on.

But, it was not the lack of food which finally resulted in a change of direction. Finn took no notice of Tufter's continuous criticism, but he couldn't ignore the lack of water which caused the tongues of the whelps to swell so much that they could no longer close their jaws. Throughout one weary night the pack loped along in dogged silence towards the south west, their eyes alert in search of game. Then, as the brazen sun once more thrust its heat on the baked earth, the pack slowed to a halt; Black Tip drew Finn's attention to a pair of Native Companions.

The bigger of the two cranes stood just over one and a half metres high. His fine blue plumage covered enough flesh to feed several dingoes. Yet it was not so much for food but, rather, as a sign that water was not too far away that Black Tip welcomed the sight of the cranes.

For some distance the country had been less arid, and now the wiry scrub allowed the pack to melt into cover, in the misty light of the coming day. For the first time, Finn witnessed the strange dance of the Native Companion. To and fro, up and down beneath their scraggy gum the two cranes footed a sort of grotesque minuet. While the cranes danced, Finn and the dingoes advanced through the scrub like snakes moving in their sleep. Not a leaf or a twig made comment on their passage as they slithered inch by inch down the morning breeze.

The prancing dance of the cranes – who mate for life and are deeply devoted to one another – was drawing to a close when death came to them both like a bolt from the heavens. It was such a death as one would choose, leaving no time for fear or grief at separation. Their necks were torn apart before they realised they were no longer alone. This time, Finn was less generous then usual; perhaps he realised his great bulk needed more sustenance than an ordinary dingo. Until he was satisfied, Finn ate rapidly and growled ominously when any other head but Warrigal's came too close.

Less than half an hour later the pack was scrambling down the banks of a river bed. In the centre, surrounded by half a kilometre or more of shingle, was a chain of small yellow puddles. Finn and Warrigal chose a good size pool to tackle, driving off with angry snarls two youngsters who tried to join them. Where the pack drank they rested, so reluctant were they to leave the precious liquid. But the memory of wild folk is short in such matters. They drank many times during the day, but when night fell they prepared to move away. By chance, a mob of kangaroos on the north bank of the river led the pack northwards and a little westerly once more.

27

The trail of man

Exactly two weeks later, the pack turned in its tracks, desperate to find the shingly river bed where some trace of moisture might remain.

In that fortnight, the pack had been decimated. All the six whelps were gone, and old Tufter and the eldest of the females were no more. Neither the carrion crows nor the ants benefited from these deaths; the pack had not hastened the end of any of its members but it had left only bones behind. Now, when any of the gaunt, dry-lipped survivors stumbled, a dozen pairs of hungry eyes glittered and a dozen pairs of lips curled away from as many sets of fangs.

The pack was starving. Many times, the thought of turning back crossed Finn's mind but still he pressed on, having no way of knowing he was in a country of vast and waterless distances. But after a fortnight's travel in which food had been scarce and water even more so, he turned in his tracks. What liquid they did find would never have been called water by men-folk. Here and there they found patches of mud in an old water hole. In other places they burrowed deep in the hot sand with feet and nose and sucked up the moisture. For the first time in his life, Finn tried to relieve his hunger by gnawing at the dry roots of trees.

All the dingoes had changed remarkably in appearance. Even Warrigal's fine coat had lost every trace of gloss and the iron-grey hairs in Finn's coat looked more like stiff bristles. His once square back was hollow and his skin swung loose over ribs that could be counted. No animal with flesh on bone and blood in veins would have been too big or fierce for the pack to attack, for hunger and thirst had made them desperate.

It was Black Tip who called a sudden halt on the second day of their return journey. He sniffed long and hard at the ground before raising his head and glaring out into the afternoon sunlight. His whimpers brought the rest of the pack eagerly around him. One by one they exchanged glances as they too caught a hint of the scent Black Tip had discovered. Had the scent been wallaby or kangaroo, the pack would have been off in pursuit without a pause. True, there was evidence of four-footed animals, but it was merged with the scent against which most wild folk draw the line: the scent of man.

In ordinary circumstances the pack would have made off in the opposite direction at the first sign of man. But these were far from ordinary times. The man-trail was the trail of living flesh, of warm animal life. At the thought of food – whether dog or man – a little moisture found its way into each dry mouth.

Compared with their need for food and drink, everything in the world became insignificant. Their hatred and fear of man was blotted out by the drive to survive. Finn, of course, had connected men with food all his life. And now he was starving. His thoughts can hardly have been the same as the dingoes' but they moved him in the same direction none the less. Without a moment's hesitation the pack loped off towards the south-east, turning away diagonally from their old track.

As the trail became warmer, the leader was conscious of conflicting emotions. There was now more of the wolf than the dog in him. Finn was well and truly a part of the wild folk. Over and above the wild folk's natural mistrust of man, Finn had the additional resentment brought about by his torture and humiliation at the camp-fire. But Finn's sense of smell was not as sharp as the dingoes', therefore, he was not so keenly conscious that he was on the trail of man. He knew it; but not with the same depth of appreciation that Warrigal or Black Tip had.

Every now and again the scent would be stronger, perhaps at some point where the men had stopped. The distinct human whiff disturbed him a great deal. He wanted nothing to do with men but there was nothing inside him stronger at that moment than the craving for food and water.

When night fell the trail was very fresh. A quarter of an hour later, the breeze brought news of a fire not far ahead. Instantly, images of the night he was driven out by burning branches flashed through Finn's mind. The pack advanced slowly and extremely cautiously. Within a few minutes the campsite was in view. Two men, tired and dejected, were stretched out beneath a twisted tree, its branches long since dead and stripped of bark. Alongside them was a large fox terrier.

The pack drew in as close as the scrub allowed. Suddenly, a slight sound from one of them had the fox terrier on his feet and barking furiously as he rushed at the scrub. In a crescent formation, the pack drew back perhaps a dozen paces, saliva dribbling down their chops. The terrier plunged into the darkness, valiantly hopping the first low bushes. It was Black Tip who pinned him to the ground and Warrigal whose fangs closed round his body. But Finn's fangs smashed the terrier in half, signalling the pack to surge over the remains in a frenzy. By the time one of the men rose and moved toward the scrub to investigate, not a hair or bone of the terrier remained – nothing except his leather collar.

Only one man had troubled to rise at all. While the pack withdrew he searched the scrub for fifteen minutes. Finding the terrier's collar he walked back to the fire and told his companion that Jock had been carried off by dingoes. The other man merely grunted wearily and rolled over on his side. Moving painfully, the first man put more wood on the fire and stretched out, waiting for sleep.

During the night, the pack scoured every inch of the scrub within a two kilometre radius. Their only reward was a few grubs and insects, which seemed to do nothing but increase their hunger. In the hours preceding dawn, the dingoes took up a watching position overlooking the sleeping men and their almost extinguished fire. What they were seeking is hard to say. As well as connecting men-folk with guns and traps, they were also connected with food and sheep. When daylight came and one of the men stirred, the pack fell back respectfully. There was no anger or cruelty in their hearts, just an overpowering desire for food.

The first man rose slowly, stretching the stiffness from his aching frame. His face under ten days growth of beard was haggard and gaunt. His ragged clothes hung from his thin body. Under the bronze tan there was a pallor which comes from lack of nourishment but in his dark-rimmed, sunken eyes there was a curious glitter, not unlike the glitter in the eyes of the wild folk who had been watching him through the night.

Presently he woke his companion. 'Time we were on the move, old chap,' he said. 'We can't afford to wait.'

The other man sat up. 'By God, I don't know whether we can afford to do anything else!' he said bitterly. 'And us carrying a fortune. I said I'd never had good luck before and I was right. Good fortune's not for the likes of me!'

'Oh, yes, it is,' the first man replied with forced cheerfulness. 'You wait till we get our legs under a dining-table, then you'll tell another tale. Come on, let's eat and get on. I think you're right about parting. We'll toss to see who goes east and who goes south. You mark my words, one of us will strike something before nightfall. Buck up Jeff, old man, this'll be our last day of hunger.'

Jeff stood up and carefully uncorked a water bottle. Each man filled his mouth, swished the water round his tongue and then let the contents slowly trickle down his parched throat. This one mouthful of water lasted several minutes and accounted for their breakfast.

'If we hadn't chucked the guns away we might have had roast dingo today,' said Jeff. 'In fact I'm not sure

I couldn't eat the brute raw. You're sure it was dingoes that got Jock?'

'I don't see what else it could have been,' said the other man. 'As for the guns, you know it was them or the stuff.'

'I'm not sure it's much good carrying that any longer. I reckon I'll dump mine. Sixty-six solid pounds of pin-fire and us dying for a crust! You've still got your revolver, haven't you?'

'Yes,' said the first man, 'and I think you should take it. I've got a good thick stick here and I couldn't hit a house at a dozen paces, even if I saw one.'

They gravely tossed a twig to decide on directions, then just as gravely shook hands and parted; Jeff heading south and the other man east. From the scrub, all but Finn watched hungrily as the men set out. He lay stretched at Warrigal's feet. Without consulting anyone, Black Tip and four others followed Jeff's trail. As it happened, Warrigal had her eyes on the other man. Nudging Finn to follow she took to the trail.

Just as the men had separated, so too had the dingoes. But being broad daylight, none of them wanted to get too close to their quarries. They merely followed, muzzles held low, their eager eyes searching for anything that might make a meal. In the meantime, the warm trail ahead of them kept hope and excitement alive.

28

In the last ditch

In the harsh midday heat, the man heading due east abandoned his swag. He'd rested for the best part of an hour directly after noon when he'd had two swigs of water – one before the rest and one afterwards. While he rested, so too did the half-pack led by Finn. Two of the dingoes watched with interest as the man buried his swag beneath a solitary, drought-seared iron-bark. No sooner was the man out of sight than the bag was unearthed with quick, vicious strokes and laid bare in the full blaze of the afternoon sun. In seconds, the canvas was ripped to shreds but their disappointment was bitter when they found only jagged bits of mineral.

Then, within a few hours, the man lost the last remnants of hope. The dingoes didn't reason about this but they felt his resignation and it gave them great satisfaction, not out of any cruelty, but simply because their meal was all the closer. The man's course was erratic, his feet dragging at every step. The pack were not alone in recognising the man's sorry plight. A flock of seven carrion crows circled the air above, sometimes swooping within metres of his head, cawing in a half-threatening, half-pleading manner.

When evening came, no fire lit the darkness. The man sat with his back against a tree. Now and again sounds came from his lips and occasionally he would fling his arms around or strike the ground with his heavy stick. Having looked but found no food, the pack moved in closer than ever to watch the man.

Finn kept his distance. Certainly he was desperate to eat, but every instinct was against him regarding the man himself as food.

The man slept in snatches and when he did, Warrigal and some of the others would creep even closer. Only when the man stirred or waved his arms in his sleep did they slink back once more. Towards dawn, Warrigal set up a long howl, waking the man with a start. One by one the rest of the pack followed Warrigal's example. Staggering to his feet, the man flung a piece of rotten wood in their direction. The pack retreated the best part of one hundred metres, snarling in a kind of wistful disappointment at finding the man still capable of so much action.

The man's cry of defiance reached Finn's ears. It was the first human sound he had heard since being driven from the boundary rider's camp. The memories awoken by the angry sounds were of torture and tyranny. Finn growled low in his throat, very fiercely. Yet, what thrilled him most was the conflict of emotions battling for supremacy in his mind; the warring between respect for man's authority and his newly-acquired wildness. The struggle between instinct and emotion was so strong that it almost overcame the furious hunger which had driven him to chew savagely on the tough dry fibrous roots between his two fore-paws.

After defiantly throwing the branch, the man sank once more to the ground. This time, his posture was ominous. On the strength of it, three of the crows that had followed him all day settled within a dozen paces with an air which suggested they would not have too much longer to wait.

When daylight came, Warrigal and the others were closer than ever, hidden in the scrub only forty paces from the man. The crows preened their funeral plumage full of bright-eyed expectancy. The pitiless sun slowly crept clear of its bed on the horizon, thrusting out keen blades of heat heralding another blazing day of drought.

Presently, a long spear of light found its way between the man's arm and face. He turned on his side, the message from the sun urging him once more on his way. Painfully, the man tried to stand but rose only to his knees before dropping forward with a groan. The crows cocked their head in interest. The dingoes also felt that, at last, the man was down for good. The bravest of the crows hopped towards the man's back. Warrigal crept forward, icicles of saliva hanging from her jaws.

Finn saw Warrigal's movements and knew exactly what they meant. His heart and mind were at once gripped by two opposing inclinations: respect for and dislike of man told him to stay where he was; hunger and his position as pack leader impelled him to join his mate. Before his eyes, the pack were closing in for the kill. And he, the unquestioned leader and master was . . .

In a second, Finn bounded forward, angrily thrusting his great shoulders between Warrigal and the big male dingo who had dared to usurp Finn's place as leader. For an instant the pack paused no more than twenty paces from the man, who raised himself slightly on to one elbow. This movement made all but Finn draw back. Warrigal snarled savagely, warning the man of his danger. With an effort, he pushed himself to his knees, grabbing his long stick as he did. Again Warrigal snarled, this time a snarl which announced the coming of a kill. It was not for others to kill where Finn led, yet, something held his muscles relaxed. He couldn't make that final leap. Again, Warrigal snarled as the man staggered to his feet. A great dread of being shamed ran through Finn. His mate's snarls forced him to take action but though he stepped forward it was without a spring.

By now the man was on his feet and swung round to face the pack with his long stick uplifted. At last Finn gathered his hind-quarters under him ready to put an end to this strange hunt in a desert of starvation. The Wolfhound actually did spring. But although his four feet left the ground they landed in exactly the same spot, with a shock which jarred every nerve and muscle in his massive frame. His sense of smell, never remarkable for the detail it provided, had told Finn nothing. But the Wolfhound's eyes couldn't mislead him. It took every particle of strength to check his body. But, with a sudden revulsion that stopped the beating of his heart, Finn realised that the man the pack had trailed was none other than the Man of all the world for him; the man whose person was sacred to him; the Master, whose loss had been the beginning and the cause of all the troubles the Wolfhound had ever known.

When Finn began his leap there had been the beginning of a killing snarl in his throat. Yet, as he came to earth, paralysed by his amazing discovery, the snarl became as curious a cry as any four-footed creature had ever made. It was more like human speech than that of wild folk, welling up from Finn's very soul.

At the same instant recognition came to the Master and he knew his huge assailant was no creature of the wild, no giant wolf or dingo but the Wolfhound of his own breeding and most careful, loving rearing. 'Finn, boy!' cried the Master in answer to the Wolfhound's own strange call.

But behind them was the pack, and in their eyes the leader had missed his kill; he had been weakened by fear and was now at the mercy of the man who, a moment before, was no more than food. For a dingo, nothing requires more courage than to attack a man in the open – a man erect and unafraid. But Warrigal had never lacked courage. Driven by hunger and devotion to her mate she flew at the man's shoulder with a snarl that called all of her kindred who weren't cowards to follow her lead or be for ever accursed.

Warrigal's white fangs raked down the man's coat-sleeve, leaving blood and skin where the cloth gave. For a moment Finn hesitated. Warrigal was his good mate, the mother of his dead children and loving companion. But against this, her fangs had fastened on the sacred flesh of the Master.

Next instant, even as the second largest dingo attacked the man's other flank, Finn pinned his mate to the earth and with one tremendous crunch, severed her jugular vein, spilling her blood on the parched dust. Immediately the pack realised that strange events were afoot. They had started as seven against one single man. Now they were five against two – one of which was their own leader, the great Wolf who had slain Tasman and Lupus. Under normal circumstances perhaps, the pack would have turned and run. But the drive of hunger was even stronger. One had even the taste of human flesh on his foaming lips. This was not a hunt but a fight and the pack would never turn tail alive from a fight.

The man had his back to the withered iron-bark. Besides the heavy stick, he was armed with an open knife. A fierce bitch found this out to her cost when she leaped at his throat. The great Wolfhound now warmed to his task. A tiger could hardly have evaded him. His onslaught was terrible and swift. It seemed he was slashing in five different directions at once. At this speed his fangs didn't have the time to drive deep enough for the kill but they had the blood streaming from every dingo that dared attack the Master.

For his part, the man dealt with two dingoes but even as the second died with the long knife-blade buried to its hilt in his chest, the man sank to the ground, exhausted. This drew the dingoes' attention from their leader, who in some mysterious way had become an enemy, to the fallen man who was now clearly a kill.

It was then that Finn outdid himself. Calling on every particle of reserve strength, he slew, in as many seconds, the three remaining dingoes. Just as a terrier slays a rat with a crunching bite and a shake, Finn flung the dingoes, weighing over eighteen kilograms apiece, upwards of five metres.

And then, there was a sudden and complete silence in that desert spot. Even as Finn licked the Master's blood-flecked face, the crows flew down to feed on the outlying dingo bodies. After what seemed an eternity of licking, Finn pointed his nose to the brazen sky and gave voice to a true Wolfhound howl.

29

Back from the wild

Four men were riding through the low, burnt-up scrub. Trotting along in front of them was a naked aborigine tracker.

'Blurry big warrigal bin run here!' said the tracker, stooping to examine a footprint in the dust. His practised eye picked out seven dingo tracks. He told the riders that these dingoes must be pretty hungry by now and that he didn't fancy the chances of the man they were following.

One of the riders – Jeff it was – nodded dolefully. 'I reckon all the dingoes in the country must've gone crazy,' he said. 'What with the six that were following me. But at least we know we're on the right track, finding his swag. My oath! Just think of them brutes scratching up a fortune like that.'

Five kilometres further on, the aborigine stopped suddenly, cupping his hand round his ear. He explained that he could hear a howling such as a big warrigal might produce. The party pressed on and in two or three minutes the white men could also hear the howling. Now, though, the tracker shook his head. That was no dingo he told them, it must be a dog.

'That's odd,' said Jeff, 'Jock was killed the night before we parted. But that's the most ungodly howl I've ever heard.'

Five minutes later, as he topped a little ridge, the tracker gave a whoop of astonishment. Lying prone on the ground was the Master with Finn sitting beside his head. One of the riders pulled out a revolver at the sight of Finn's shaggy head.

'Well I'll be jiggered,' gasped Jeff, 'what sort of beast do you call that?'

The riders galloped down the slope and flung themselves from their horses. The leading man waved his whip at Finn, driving him away. But Finn's diligent licking had finally revived the Master.

'For God's sake, don't hurt the dog. He saved my life. Killed six dingoes. God's sake, don't touch the . . .'

With that he lapsed into unconsciousness once more. While the aborigine gazed admiringly at the dingoes, Jeff propped up his friend and produced a flask of brandy. Although Finn's hackles were raised and his lips drawn back, he was aware that the Master was being helped.

The party had food and water a plenty and it wasn't long before the Master was sitting up and munching soaked bread. Someone tossed a crust to Finn and seeing the way he bolted it down, realised the hound must also be close to starving. After Finn devoured his first meal in days, the Master called him over and weakly put his arm round Finn's bony shoulders while he told his companions how Finn had fought for his life and how they knew each other so well.

Exactly a week later, Finn lay on the balcony of a country hotel, his nose resting on the Master's knee. Beside the Master sat the Mistress of the Kennels who now and again caressed Finn's head. Finn was still thin but he had regained his strength. His eyes gleamed as bright as ever through his overhanging eaves of iron-grey hair.

'Well,' said the Master, 'it takes some time to become used to being rich. I suppose we are rich. They say the claim is good for six fortunes long after we've spent our first.' (The sixty odd pounds of opal he had been carrying had sold for £21,250).

'One thing I do know for sure is that there isn't the money in all of Australia that would make me part with Finn again. Hey, boy!'

The Wolfhound raised his bearded muzzle and softly licked the Master's thin brown hand. No doubt it was his weakness that brought a kind of wetness to the man's eyes.

'It's Sussex by the sea for us, old friend. As soon as I'm fit and well again, in another month or so. And God willing, that's where we shall spend the rest of our days!'

As Finn responded in his own way to the Master's reassurance there was little trace of wildness in the great Wolfhound's eyes.